HOOP CITY

BY

SCOTT BLUMENTHAL
AND
BRETT HODUS

www.scobre.com

Scobre Press Corporation
2255 Calle Clara
La Jolla, CA 92307

Scobre Press books may be purchased for educa-
tional, business or sales promotional use.

First Scobre edition published 2002.

Edited by Ramey Temple
Illustrated by Larry Salk
Cover Design by Michael Lynch

ISBN 0-9741695-6-0

HOME RUN EDITION

www.scobre.com

CHAPTER ONE

FIFTEEN HOURS

"I'm on your wing, T. On your wing if you need me."

I always knew where my brother Mike was on the basketball court. "Right here, Tony!" Mike shouted, giving another wave. I slowed my dribble as I reached a faded yellow three-point arc. The defense came closer.

Two defenders blocked my path. They swiped for a steal, but missed. I dribbled as fast as I could in between and around them. A voice from beyond the court shouted, "Pass the ball, showboat!"

I picked up my dribble. When I looked up, Mike was streaking toward the basket. I lofted an alley-oop pass at the rim. Mike left his feet and glided toward the hoop. He grabbed the pass in mid-air, and slammed the basketball home.

The rim rattled as Mike let go. He landed on his feet with the backboard shaking. That tired rim wouldn't have to worry about Mike after today. My brother and I were leaving in the morning to attend the University of New York.

Every day, Harlem's future stars lined up for a chance to play here. And every day, they went home disappointed. Mike and I owned these courts. But the time had come for us to leave them. Tomorrow, someone else would have a chance to win at the "Jungle."

They call these courts the Jungle because out here, you've got to fight to survive. This is where the best players in New York City develop. It happens right here in Harlem, a place where life isn't easy. The usual crowd stood around the fence during our last game before college. Some of these guys were one-time great players who had wasted college scholarships and NBA dreams. They had messed around with drugs and crime and never made it back. Now they were lost, wondering where their dreams went.

Mike and I watched each other carefully. We refused to get trapped on the wrong side of the fence. We're twin brothers, born two minutes apart. We've been partners since before we could dribble straight. My name is Tony Hope, but people around here call me "T." People say my brother and I are gonna play in the NBA someday. Tomorrow morning we leave for college. Leaving here is gonna be the greatest and saddest thing that's ever happened to me. I love

Harlem. I just hate what it does to people.

After Mike's dunk, we shuffled back on defense. I bent my knees and pulled on my shorts. I was ready for oncoming traffic. Mike slapped his hands onto the concrete, "One-nothing! Play some D!"

I was guarding Bo Johnson, a skinny point guard who never seemed to miss. He was using his body to separate me from the ball as he dribbled. Bo's biggest problem was that he couldn't dribble left. I slid over toward his right. Bo faked left and tried to beat me. I was ready and waiting. I knocked the ball from his hands. He complained that he'd been fouled, but his whining was aimed at the back of my head. I was already off and running. Nothing stood between me and the basket.

Mike was trailing me on the fast break. "Behind you, T!" I knew exactly what to do. I pretended to go in for the lay up. Instead of scoring, I bounced the ball high off the backboard. I watched Mike soar to the hoop. He grabbed the ball with his right hand and slammed it home.

The crowd began shaking the fence again. "Did you see that? He was three feet above the rim!"

Mike and I bumped chests as the ball bounced below us. We dared Bo to pick it up. Mike grabbed me by the shirt. "How's anyone gonna stop us?" I smiled from ear to ear, picturing our bright future clearly.

We went on to win that game, 11-3. Bo Johnson threw the ball at my chest. He was a sore loser. "Didn't we make a rule that you and your brother couldn't play together?"

Mike walked up to Bo confidently. He palmed Bo's tiny head. "I don't remember that rule. Do you T?"

"Nope, I don't remember that rule either." I threw the ball back to Bo. "Who's got next over here? The Hope brothers are done."

Mike and I stepped off the court together for the last time. We moved toward a bench beyond the courts. Xavier White walked toward us. "Make us proud, fellas." He shook our hands and walked away. A few more guys wished us luck. These were the same guys we'd played with since we were kids. That was back when they used to call me "Shorty."

We started to watch the next game. Our world was changing. But life in Harlem would remain the same. A gust of wind flung trash through the holes in the metal links around the courts. Younger players bounced up and down, stretching their legs. They were ready to prove themselves. Tomorrow, things would be the same at the Jungle, only Mike and I wouldn't be there.

"It's crazy saying goodbye. To be honest, I don't want to leave this place." Mike stared into space as a few more guys passed by. "I wish they had a college in Harlem with a good hoops team. I'd play here in a second." Mike was nervous about leaving home. In eighteen years, we'd barely left New York. Life had been simple until now.

With college fifteen hours away, things were about to get even more complex. For me, leaving home was something I looked forward to. Getting closer to my NBA dream was all I ever thought about. For Mike though, things were different. Don't get me wrong, he loved basketball too. He was the captain of our team, and the best player in the state. He'd also been prom king and earned varsity letters in three sports. Teachers loved him and he was the most popular kid in school. I guess it's the way he carries himself. People in Harlem followed my brother like he was a movie star. So when Mike told me he didn't want to leave, I understood.

I stared into the street and tried to ease Mike's worries. "You think life is good now, just wait until we're in the NBA." I smiled.

Steam rose up from the streets. The August heat had taken over. Mike walked over to a hot dog vendor, paid the man a dollar, and slapped him five. Then he swallowed down a dog in two bites. He walked back toward me, mustard running off his bottom lip. "This is home, you know? One last night in a place we've spent our entire lives. Let's make it a night to remember." Mike spoke with a spark in his eyes.

"What do you mean?" I'd seen that expression before. Like when we were eleven and he had convinced me to sneak out. We shot hoops for an hour in the middle of winter. We both got so sick that we missed two weeks of school. And Mom punished us for two more weeks after that. I also saw that look on Mike's face when Tommy Hillson called me "stupid." Mike broke Tommy's nose with a left hook. That mistake grounded us another two weeks.

My brother had been getting me punished my whole life. And it always started with that look. I knew it meant trouble.

I repeated myself. "What do you mean? What are you gonna do?"

He grinned. "I'm going to a party tonight. You should come."

I was never one for parties. "I don't know. I've gotta pack."

"Pack? Come on! Who knows, maybe you'll have some fun."

I had a hard time saying no to my brother. "OK. Who's going?"

He paused. "Well, Nick and Devon are—"

I cut him off. "I'm not going anywhere with those guys. You shouldn't either."

"I'm doing what I'm doing, T. You can come if you want." Mike bumped knuckles with me and walked away. Fifty yards later, he stopped. He wagged his finger at me, "Make sure you're in bed by ten, mister." We laughed as he turned the corner for home.

I stayed to watch the last game of the day. I

couldn't understand why Mike was going to a party with those morons. I wasn't going with him. That was for sure.

It was five o'clock and the sun began to hide behind the taller buildings. I wanted it to be morning. In fifteen hours Mike and I would be sitting in our dorm room at UNY. I couldn't wait. I bounced up from my seat, ready to begin the next chapter of my life.

Four blocks later I approached our East Harlem apartment. Climbing eight flights of stairs every day helped strengthen my calves. When I reached our place I pulled out my keys and chipped away some splintered wood from our door. Mom complained to the landlord about the door, but he never fixed anything.

Mike beat me home by a few minutes. He and Mom were sitting on the couch when I walked in. I bent over to drop Mom a kiss on my way to the kitchen. I grabbed an apple and took a bite. My cheeks were stuffed when my brother made a stupid face at me. I almost spit a pile of apple onto the floor.

I stared out the kitchen window, thinking about college. The streets had turned black. *The night was approaching.*

I was startled by a knock at the door. Mike jumped up, expecting company. When he opened the door, Nick Cipro and Devon Jacox were standing there wearing backpacks. Nick was tall with an athletic build. He had dropped out of high school a year earlier. Drinking and drugs had taken over his life. Devon was a scrawny guy who had a high pitched laugh like a hyena. He'd also dropped out of school. These were not the people I wanted hanging around my brother.

I slapped hands with Nick and Devon. I bit my lip to stop myself from telling them to leave. I didn't want these guys in my house, taking my brother off to some party. The mood in the room was calm, but I wasn't. Devon made a funny comment and Mom laughed. My eyes locked with Mike's. I slowly shook my head from side to side. I spoke without saying a word: "Stay here tonight, Mike. We'll talk about UNY and pack our stuff. Me and you tonight, Hope."

It was just a few moments before the guys began heading out of the apartment. Nick and Devon wondered why I wasn't coming. I said that I wanted to get a good night's sleep. The truth was, I wanted no part of their plans. Mike followed his 'friends' out. I slapped my brother's hand before he left.

I stared out the peephole, watching him disappear down the stairs. Mike even walked like an all-star, chin up, smooth steps, never a change of pace. People said that when all was said and done, he would be the best basketball player to ever come out of Harlem. I always knew my brother was a better player than me. My job was easy. If he was open, I passed him the ball. If he was covered, I set a pick for him. If he took a bad shot, I battled for the rebound.

The telephone rang as Mike disappeared down the stairs. The voice on the other end was panicked. "It's Lloyd. Where's Mike?"

Lloyd Bright was a friend of ours from school. "He just left with Nick and Devon. What's up?"

"I talked to Perry and he said that party was going to be crazy tonight."

"What do you mean by crazy?" I asked.

Lloyd was quick. "You know what I mean. The kind of party you go to if you're looking for trouble."

My heart jumped. "What should I do?"

"I don't know, man. But I'd get Mike." Lloyd was serious.

"Where's the party?" I spoke while I changed into a pair of jeans.

"I'm not sure. Perry says it's somewhere over by the high school." His answer was vague.

I hung up the phone and laced up my sneakers. "Mom, I'm going to meet Mike."

Mom responded from her bedroom. "I thought you said you were going to get a good night's sleep."

"I will." I tried to hide any panic in my voice. "I gotta go, Mom." If I kept talking, I'd lose track of Mike.

"Be home by eleven-thirty."

I left the apartment, locking the door behind me. My last night in Harlem was going to be differ-

ent than I'd imagined. I wanted to be in my bed, dreaming about UNY. Instead, I was racing out of our building as fast as I could. I reached the bottom of the stairs and noticed the guys walking toward the river. I followed them from a block behind.

After a few blocks they had reached Jenkins Park, better known in Harlem as the "Park." This was where kids shot hoops before they earned an invite to the Jungle. I stopped for a second and remembered back when I played on these beat up courts. The holes we'd cut out of the fence years ago seemed to have shrunk in size, maybe I'd just gotten bigger.

On the far backboard, the letters 'LW' were written. I knew those initials, Lamar Williams, Harlem's greatest player. You couldn't walk ten steps in Harlem without hearing about Lamar Williams and the legend of his "Sweet Feet."

Mike and I were once great players at the Park. But you're not a legend like "Sweet Feet" until you beat the best. This was our journey. And it all began six years earlier, right here, through the holes in the Park fence...

CHAPTER TWO

SHORTY

It was a perfect spring day for a sixth grader. The weather caused the Jungle courts to be crowded that day. So some guys who usually played up there, walked six blocks to beat up on us kids at the Park.

I passed through a hole in the fence onto the blacktop at the Park. Someday, I would play on the Jungle courts. But first, I had to prove myself here. The kind of basketball at the Park was typical Harlem hoops: Always tough, always fast paced, and always filled with trash talk. I tried not to talk too much, Mike did enough jawing for the both of us.

While I stretched, a figure approached. He was tall and wore his hair in dreadlocks. "What's up, Hope?" He spoke confidently.

"What's up?" I replied, not sure who he was. "Do I know you?"

"Oh, *my bad*. You're not Mike Hope. You look like this kid I know." Mike had hit a growth spurt and was a full four inches taller than me. Somehow, people still had a hard time telling us apart.

A smaller friend of "dreadlocks" reached up to tap him on the shoulder. "That's "Shorty." Mike Hope's little brother." I hated that nickname and I hated being thought of us Mike's younger brother.

"Actually, I'm Tony. Mike's my twin." A lot of guys knew Mike. He was one of the top young players in Harlem.

The taller guy shook my hand. "I'm Jason, Jason Helms. You better know that name, Shorty." He rose his eyebrows in a cocky way. I *did* know that name. Jason used to play and dominate, here at the Park. He'd been playing up at the Jungle for the past two years. "Tell your brother we need a fifth guy today."

After he realized I wasn't Mike, he lost interest in speaking with me. He made his way toward his friends. I didn't want to waste this opportunity. "Uh…Mike's coming later, but I can play until he gets here."

"No, Shorty." He turned around. "When your brother comes down let me know. I'm not trying to run training sessions for kids." He drew laughter from his friends. "We can't have a midget running around this court." They laughed again. Jason dribbled away.

The laughter grew. My heart pounded like a war

drum. An instant later I was running full speed toward the most feared player on the court. I came up behind him and knocked the ball from his hands. I made an easy lay up and pointed at Jason. "This midget made you look like a punk—punk!"

Jason grabbed me by the shirt. The next thing I remember was his arm extending back and his fist smacking my jaw. I fell to the floor with a thump. He stood over me. "Respect your elders, punk!" He grabbed the ball back and walked away.

I wiped some blood from my lower lip. "Hey Jason!"

He turned and faced me. "What? You want some more, Shorty?" The answer was no. I definitely didn't want anymore, but a fire was burning inside me.

"You and me, one on one." I spoke before I thought. Playing against a player five inches taller, and four years older, wasn't a good idea.

"What'd you just ask me?" Jason and his friends started laughing. Once again, I was the butt of their jokes. He sat down on a bench and sipped from his water bottle. "Go home, Shorty." He wasn't taking me seriously.

"One on one, to eleven, Jason." I spit blood onto the ground. "Or are you just a punk?" Everyone moved in closer. I heard some mumbling from the crowd. I thought I was about to get hit in the face again. Or maybe I was about to get a game with the best player on the court.

Kids I knew were leaning against the fence, watching everything unfold. The court began to clear. Jason took off his shirt and revealed an upper body that was twice the size of mine. I took my shirt off and it was not a pretty sight. My ribs stuck out and my arms were puny.

Jason walked toward me and threw the ball at my chest. "Check it up!"

I caught the ball. "Wait. If I win, you get me an invite to the Jungle."

Jason smiled. "Shorty, if you win I'll take you to the *Amazon* Jungle."

I bent down and tightened my shoelaces, cradling the ball under my left arm. Mom had taught us to be confident. So, there was no fear in my eyes. "I'm not scared of you." I spoke as I checked the ball.

Just as the game was about to start, Mike showed up. He made his way onto the court and Jason had some words for him. "Your brother's got a bigger mouth than you, Mike. I'm about to shut it for him."

Mike ignored him and came over to me. He grabbed the ball from my hands. "How'd this happen?" He pointed to my swollen lip.

"I asked for it." I didn't want Mike involved.

He yelled over at Jason anyway. "You like picking on guys half your size?"

Jason laughed. "Shorty needs another couple of inches before he's half my size."

14

"Why don't you play me, tough guy?" Mike began walking toward Jason.

I stepped in his path. "Let me handle this, Mike."

"You can handle this guy?" Mike looked over at Jason, then back at me.

I tried to grab the ball from him, but he wouldn't give it up. "Just let me play him, Mike."

Mike dropped the ball back into my hands. "OK. This guy's a baller, though, T." This was a term used to describe a talented basketball player. "You can beat him though. Don't back down." He gave me a knuckle bump and stared at Jason as he walked toward the sideline. While kids stood against the fence, a seat on the bench was saved just for Mike. He was becoming a legend on these courts.

Jason stood in front of me in a weak defensive stance. He wasn't taking me and my twelve-year-old body seriously. On the first play I blew past him left, making an easy lay-up. He wasn't too rattled. On my next possession his long arm swatted my shot easily. He regained control of the ball and stood at the top of the key. "Here it comes, Hope. Get ready."

I crouched down defensively. I would have more impact stopping the dribble than I would blocking shots. Many defenders like to watch the path of the ball. Others like to look into their opponent's eyes. I stared at the hips. An offensive player wasn't going anywhere unless his hips shifted first.

Helms began to yo-yo the ball up and down.

He noticed my strange defensive style and had an opportunity for a joke. "Any of you guys have a spatula? I think Shorty's stuck to the–" I never let him complete the insult. I sprung from my stance, knocking the ball away. I made another easy lay-up.

All of Jason's friends started jeering at him. I dribbled back to the top of the key. Suddenly he looked like a linebacker about to drill a quarterback. His nostrils were flaring and sweat dripped down his face. He charged. I turned my back and protected the ball. I felt heavy slaps on my wrists and forearms. A voice called out from the crowd. "He's foulin' the kid! Play like a man, Helms!" But Jason wouldn't let up. He was smacking and pushing with all his force. I had to do something.

After a few more bumps, I tried a play that I'd practiced against my brother. Jason's legs were spread while he smacked at the back of my arms. I turned around and bounced the ball between his open legs. Then I darted past as he lunged for the rock. "Too late!" I yelled, grabbing the ball after two bounces and rolling in another lay-up.

Jason's crew got louder. "Shorty's making you look stupid, Jay."

"Three-nothing, Hope!" Mike shouted from the sideline, a huge smile on his face.

Now a few of Jason's friends were cheering for me. "You're the man, Shorty! Show him what's up!"

Jason wisely changed his game plan after my

early advantage. I was giving away five inches and fifty pounds to the sixteen-year-old. He decided to use his size rather than his ball handling skills. When he started backing the ball into the post, I had little chance at stopping him. Bumping me backward gave him easy looks at short post shots. He began to score again and again. But I wouldn't give up. I jumped, swiped, shot, and bled my way back into the game. The score went back and forth for the next ten minutes. This was quite a battle: My quickness against his size, his pride versus my will.

We were tied at ten in a game to eleven. Jason held the ball at the top of the key. "Next hoop wins," he muttered. I tried to keep my intensity high. Jason turned his back to the basket and powered me into the post. I leaned into the middle of his back. It was all I could do to hold my ground. But it wasn't enough. Jason moved to the basket with ease. By the time he turned to face up, a three-foot bank shot was all he was left with. He faded and shot it in, nothing but net.

Helms pumped his fist in the air and nearly dropped to his knees. He was tired. I took this as a compliment. Beating a twelve-year-old by a single point should have been easy. But it wasn't. I wondered if I should have tried for the steal on the last play of the game. I wondered when I would get another chance at an invite to the Jungle.

Jason came over to me and shook my hand. "Nice game, Tony." I couldn't believe it. He called me Tony. I'd graduated. No one ever called me Shorty again. I earned Jason's respect. I could see it in his face when he approached me. He spoke again, before exiting through a hole in the fence. "You've got a ton of game, Tony. If you ever need someone to run with, come up to the Jungle. I'll play with you anytime."

I nodded my head, beaten, but respected.

CHAPTER THREE

LOCKED OUT

It was close to nine o'clock. Memories of my childhood faded as Mike, Devon, and Nick continued past the Park. When they reached an empty lot they stopped and pulled their backpacks off. I followed from about twenty yards back. I stood in the shadows behind an old fence. I could see and hear them clearly through the splintered wood.

"Guys, I'm not too sure about going to this party." Mike sounded concerned.

Devon responded. "What's the matter, college boy, you scared of fun?" Devon's hyena laugh was loud. "Still time to run home."

Mike forced a smile. He didn't fool me. I knew he was nervous. I had to find out why. One by one the guys unzipped their packs. I leaned in toward the fence, trying to get a clear view. They gathered in close. My concentration was broken by the sounds of a car. "Get down!" Devon pointed to his left, diving behind a dumpster. Mike and Nick followed.

An instant later a New York City police car rolled up to the empty lot. The street became quiet. A flashlight shined and the officer looked out her window. Mike crouched as low as he could, holding on to the side of the dumpster. His arms were shaking. His legs were buried in garbage. I sat motionless with my back to the action. Soon the flash of light disappeared. All that was left were sighs and laughter.

Less than a day away from a college basketball scholarship, Mike was ducking behind trash to avoid the law. What was he doing? He knew we had to get to the NBA and show Mom a better life. Had Mike forgotten Mom?

The guys scraped trash from their clothes. They arrived at the corner of 151st Street and 1st Avenue out of breath. They'd reached a crossroad. I thought they'd be going west, toward civilization. I was wrong. They went east, toward the river. There were only two things down there by the river: our old high school and trouble. I knew these jokers weren't going to catch up on their studies. They were looking for trouble. The stakes had been raised.

A few minutes later I stopped at the front steps of our high school. Mike was fifty feet ahead. He passed by the back door to our old gym. The con-

crete steps leading to the entrance seemed more cracked than they were a few months ago. Every window was covered with metal bars. The painted front door was two shades of ugly brown. The sign reading 'Public School 44' hung upside down. When principals and security guards went home for the summer, this was what PS-44 became.

I imagined my new life at UNY, fourteen hours and counting. Tomorrow the stairs would be perfect, the windows clean. Fresh coats of blue and orange paint would color signs for the University of New York.

I moved forward quietly. I could still hear Mike's voice up the street. Fifty feet later I was standing in front of our old gym. I tugged on a chain that locked the entrance. I remembered the first time I was locked out of that gym...

After my game against Jason Helms everything changed. Mike and I started playing at the Jungle. The buzz about us grew. In fact, the *New York Times* ran an article about us. Mike took these comments in stride. But I let the praise go to my head. Mike was used to people telling him he was great. I wasn't. When I showed up on the first day of varsity basketball tryouts, I had an attitude.

"On your wing, T. Ball, ball, ball," Mike was running alongside me on the fast break. There was only one man guarding the basket. Instead of throwing a bounce pass, I tossed up an alley-oop. The ball rose above him and bounced off the backboard. I'd blown an easy fast break.

The defender guarding me picked up the ball and sprinted down court. Coach Walter Harris glared at me. Mike hustled full speed down court to prevent an easy basket. I knew that I had a spot on varsity no matter what happened during tryouts, so I jogged.

After our opponents scored another lay-up, I dribbled up the floor. We were down by one in a game to eleven. We needed to score. This was my chance to impress Coach. I dribbled the ball over the half-court stripe, ignoring an open teammate.

The defender guarding me was slow. I could have blown by him at any time. A lay-up would have tied the game. But I wanted to show off my jump shot. Coach needed to see *all* my skills. I dribbled around the swinging arms of the defender until my body was next to Coach's. I stood four feet beyond the arc.

With a head fake forward I was able to create space between myself and my opponent. Mike saw the look in my eyes. As usual, he was there to help me. He set a strong pick. This meant that he used his body to block my defender. His pick left me with an open look at a jump shot. I squared my body to the basket. My form was flawless. I was sure my shot would be good.

I held my follow through in the air. "That's money," I said, waiting for the ball to swish. My confident smile soured. The ball ran out of gas on the way to the rim. The shot dropped short—an embarrassing air ball. I shook my head in disbelief.

The whistle blew. "Hey Hope! You always hold your follow through on air balls?" Coach Harris was furious. "Stop the game." Squeaking sneakers were silenced. All that was left was the thunder of Coach's voice. "All I see is playground in you, Hope. Play *with* your teammates, not against them!" This wasn't what I expected on the first day of tryouts. "Get some water guys."

I couldn't believe that Coach cut the game short. Everyone gathered by the bleachers. I stayed on the court. The game wasn't over yet. Mike could tell I was about to explode. He signaled me to calm down. I ignored him.

A heated discussion was taking place in my head. I'm a great player. Last week Mike and I had our pictures in the *New York Times*! Coach Harris never had his picture in the *Times*. Why was he embarrassing me? Who did he think he was? I continued my thoughts. Why is he disrespecting me?

I stood deep in thought at center court. Coach stared at me, waiting for my next move. "Are you going to join your teammates or do you have something else you'd like to say?"

I was angry. "This is the first time you've seen me play, Coach. How can you tell I'm all playground?" I raised my voice. "Either way, I got skills. You should understand that."

Coach Harris moved closer to me. My four-teen-year-old frame stood tall to face him. I wouldn't back down. "Are you telling me how to do my job, Hope?" He moved to about three inches from my ear. "I've been coaching kids like you for thirty years. You know how long that is?"

I spoke loudly. "Maybe you should retire."

His voice crashed down like lightning. "When you're in this gym, you are in *my* house!" I flinched backward. Coach, a mountain of a man, was scream-ing. "*Nobody* is gonna disrespect me in my house! You understand me?" His chest was heaving.

I didn't answer.

"I said do you understand me?"

I deliberately paused. "Yeah, whatever," I said nonchalantly.

Mike walked onto the court. "Coach, can I say something?"

"Go back with your teammates, Michael! Your brother owes me an apology." Mike sat down with the guys.

Coach stared at me. "Well?"

I remember thinking that I had to establish my-self. Coach needed me for the next four years. He was going to respect my game whether he liked it or not. I looked up at him. "Coach, I think the only per-son who needs to apologize is you. You disrespected me in front of my teammates."

Coach shrugged his shoulders. "OK. If that's how you want to do it, get out of here. I'm the guy blowing the whistle, not you." He pointed his finger at me. "You have no respect. You're not welcome anywhere near this gym. So collect your stuff and get out."

I stepped back. Had I just been thrown off the team? My hands shook as I grabbed my bag from a hook on the back wall. I approached the exit and turned around before leaving. "You've got no idea who you're sending home." Everyone was silent, staring. I couldn't look at my brother. I put my backpack on my shoulder and left. When I closed the door to the gym that day, it locked behind me.

CHAPTER FOUR

SWEET FEET

  I continued past my old gym, following the guys down 151st Street. One block away was the building Lamar "Sweet Feet" Williams grew up in. When I was in grade school we used to come down to his apartment every day. We'd stand on each other's shoulders to get a look into his second story window. We were his biggest fans. Though Lamar has long since moved out, his apartment is a reminder of his place in Harlem's history.

  When the guys approached the building, Nick pointed toward Lamar's window. I waited for Mike. Normally he'd stand on the tips of his toes to catch a glimpse into the legend's apartment. He'd move his head from side to side to get different viewpoints. He desperately wanted to be known as Harlem's greatest basketball player—the title currently owned by

"Sweet Feet."

On this night, Mike didn't look up. In fact, he avoided Lamar's place. He'd missed the coolest sight in all of Harlem. In that window hangs a pair of size twelve sneakers. The same pair "Sweet Feet" wore for every game he played at Public School 44. They hung as a tribute, they added to his legend. The shoelaces dangled, the tongue was ripped. The sole was worn and the color had faded from white to gray. Every time I saw those old shoes I felt a tap on the shoulder. Sometimes I heard them whisper, "You can do it, Tony."

I crept closer to the guys, afraid to lose them around the next corner. Dim streetlights blurred my vision. My tired eyes squinted through the haze to get a better look at the sneakers.

"Tony!" A voice rang out from the darkness.

I jumped back as Mike approached. "What are you doing here?" He asked.

I guess I wasn't cut out to be a spy. I'd been busted. "I...um..."

The guys joined Mike. "What is this, a family reunion?"

Mike moved closer to me. "I thought you didn't want to come with us, T."

I snapped. "I don't know where you idiots are taking Mike. But I've got a bad feeling about this party. Lloyd said that—"

Nick burst out laughing. "Lloyd said! That

guy's more uptight than you, Tony."

I ignored Nick. "Let's go home, Mike. We start college tomorrow, remember? We still have to pack and—"

Devon butted in. "You can pack in the morning can't you, Mike?"

Mike answered. "Yeah, I can pack tomorrow, T."

I stared at my brother. "Make your own decision, Mike. We've worked too hard for you to get into trouble the night before—"

Devon cut me off again. "What trouble? It's a party! You ever leave the Jungle long enough to go to a party?"

Mike put his hand on Devon's chest. "Shut up, Devon."

I shot a look at my brother. "I'm asking you to come home with me."

Nick put his arm on Mike's shoulder. "Let's go, Mike, be your own man."

Nick and Devon started walking down 151st. I stood on the sidewalk, staring at my twin brother backpedaling away from me. "Everything's cool, T. Go home and get some sleep. I'll be fine." I watched Mike get smaller and smaller. A feeling of helplessness overcame me. The time for spying was over. I started the long walk home alone.

I remembered the last time I was spying. Back then, I wasn't looking for Mike. I was looking for my *spot on the varsity basketball team...*

Two and a half months after being kicked out of Coach Harris's gym, I started to miss basketball. I'd been working over at Soapy Sid's Car Wash. The only way I kept my game sharp was by firing towels into buckets. If towel basketball ever became a sport, I'd be a pro for sure. Aside from a little fun, working at the car wash was hard. When I came home at night, my hands would barely be able to hold a basketball. But they *were* able to sneak twenty dollar bills into Mom's purse. This was the one thing that made me smile in my new life without hoops.

One Tuesday afternoon I came home early from work. Mom's heavy breathing filled the living room. She was sound asleep, her purse on the floor next to her. I didn't want to turn the light on and wake her. I crept through the darkness, to Mom's side. I reached into my pocket and pulled out a wad of cash. Then I unzipped Mom's bag, dropping some in. "Tony, what are you doing in my purse?" I jumped back. Mom had been awake the whole time. "I've been noticing extra money in my wallet. Have you ever seen me with extra money?" She sat upright, her expression turned serious. "I know what you've been doing. You're a good boy, Tony."

I sat down next to my mother, who rubbed my back lovingly. She reached into her bag and handed me a bunch of money. Every dollar I had given her for the past two months. She hadn't spent a penny. "This is your money. You earned it. After your father left us…" She paused. Mom never talked about him. "I knew life would be tough. But I never asked for your help paying bills. That's my job. Your job's to go after your dreams."

"I just wanted to help." I rested my head on Mom's shoulder.

She kissed my forehead. "You need to go back to playing basketball. That's what makes you happy." She stood up. "Now I've *really* got to get some sleep." She laughed as she made her way into her bedroom. "Always could fake you out."

Mom was right. I needed basketball. Varsity practice was about to start and I was going. These would be my first steps on a basketball court since my run in with Coach Harris. The team was only a few days away from its first-round playoff game against Hamilton High. With me on the couch, the chances of hanging up a state championship banner had disappeared. The guys needed me.

When I arrived at school, I walked to the gym. I could hear bouncing balls in the background. "Come on guys, hustle!" Coach Harris's voice jolted me. I peeked around the corner at the entrance to the gym. The door was cracked open. I grabbed the handle, trying to spy without being noticed.

Mike congratulated his teammates after scoring the winning hoop in a scrimmage. Five other guys walked over to the water fountain. My ear pressed closer to the action. "Well done, Michael." Coach Harris was pleased. "You guys are starting to come together now."

I wanted a piece of that game, but my pride kept me from walking in and apologizing. Through the slit in the door, I watched half of practice. They *were* coming together. In between jumpers and rebounds Mike laughed with his friends. Teammates slapped five and bumped knuckles. Mom was right. I did miss basketball, only basketball didn't seem to miss me. PS-44 didn't need Tony Hope. I couldn't watch practice anymore. I left, broken.

I came home later that night and found my brother messing with our old television set. He was trying to get a clear picture for the start of the game. I felt like I hadn't seen Mike in weeks. We slapped hands. "What's up, T? How's Soapy Sid's?" Mike smiled at me as I took a bite of his sandwich.

I spoke with my mouth full. "It's all right." I swallowed. "How's the team?"

"Decent. But we've got no point guard. I'm trying to win a state championship and you're washing cars."

I changed the subject. "TV broken again?"

"That thing's always busted." Mike grabbed his sandwich away from me.

The television reception slowly began to improve. I leaned forward. "There's something I want to talk to you about. I know you're waiting for me to apologize to Coach Harris. But it's not gonna happen."

Mike spoke with half a sandwich stuffed in his cheeks. "What do you mean it's not gonna happen? You know how bad I need you out there? Dizzy's playing the point. He's making *me* dizzy."

I sat down next to Mike. "Dizzy's running the point?" Dizzy was a player I had schooled for years at the playground.

Mike swallowed. "You've got to apologize. If you don't, you can forget about next year."

I couldn't look at him. "What if I don't want to play next year?"

"You don't want to play?" Mike sat up sharply and clicked the television off. "Tony, we were supposed to be the two best players in Harlem. One argument with a coach and you're finished? Don't you still love this game?"

"Coach Harris disrespected me."

"Who cares? I asked you a question, do you still love basketball?"

I stared at the floor. "Of course I still love basketball."

Mike stood up. "Good. I have something for you. If you said you didn't love basketball, I was gonna take Dizzy."

I followed him. "Take Dizzy where? What do you got?" Mike didn't answer, tiptoeing through the hallway past Mom's room.

We stepped into our bedroom and he opened the top drawer of his dresser. "You're really not going to apologize to Coach? I shouldn't even be giving you this." He handed me a pair of tickets.

My eyes widened when I saw the logo of the New York Pride. Somehow, Mike had gotten us tickets for Lamar Williams's final game at Towers Memorial Arena. The game had been sold out for months. "How'd you get these?" I asked.

He dropped the tickets on the dresser. "Are you through with basketball or do you want to see 'Sweet Feet?'

The nickname "Sweet Feet" was earned on the streets of Harlem. Back when Lamar was thirteen people would come from all over just to watch him dribble. During his four years at PS-44, the legend of Lamar Williams grew. By the time he graduated, every kid in New York had heard of his "Sweet Feet."

Twisting our antenna was the only way I got to watch my favorite player. Although the reception was fuzzy, I always tuned in. I loved when he crossed over on an opponent or hit a game-winning shot. We watched every game we could. So how could I pass up a trip to watch him play in person?

Two weeks later, Mike and I were six rows deep in the stands at Towers Memorial. I sat upright, watching the greatest basketball player in the world in his final game. Once the ball tipped, I stopped thinking about my troubles. I just watched "Sweet Feet."

Lamar played great that night. Even at thirty seven, his feet danced like he was a kid. Aging knees and a bad back had forced him to retire. But the way he moved that night, you would have thought he could play forever.

After the game, Mike and I waited outside the Pride locker room for "Sweet Feet." There were probably close to fifty of us kids lining the tunnel. Forty-five minutes later, a security guard emerged, clearing a path. Out of the darkness came a familiar smile. Lamar Williams stood three feet away from us. He was dressed in a light brown suit.

He stood tall above the crowd. Kids tugged at his side, begging for autographs. One even wrapped himself around Lamar's enormous leg. "Sweet Feet" laughed calmly, the youngster still attached. "Hey guys, give me some space and I'll get to all of you. I'll sign for everyone."

People bullied for position as Mike and I watched a line form in front of us. The dust settled and we were dead last. Lamar signed autographs for everyone in line. Twenty minutes later, our moment arrived. "We're going to miss you Mr. Williams." I shook his hand firmly as I spoke.

Mike shook next. "My brother and I grew up watching you play. It's gonna be tough watching the Pride without you."

"Thanks guys." Lamar grabbed two five-by-eight photos of himself from a box. "Who should I sign these to?"

Mike introduced us. "I'm Mike Hope and this is my brother Tony."

Lamar's eyes lit up. "You're not the Hope brothers from Harlem, are you?"

I was shocked that Lamar Williams knew us. "How'd you know that?"

"I read that article about you two. Said you guys could play some ball. How'd the season go?"

Mike spoke because I couldn't. "It went OK. We lost a tough one to Carver in the quarterfinals. We'll get them next year—if we can get this guy back on the team." I tried to smile along with Mike.

"Sweet Feet's" head shifted toward me. "What do you mean, *back* on the team?" His gaze was intense. "Why were you off the team in the first place?"

I hung my head as I spoke. "I had an argument with Coach Harris and decided I didn't want to play for him."

"What do you mean *you* decided? That's not your choice." Lamar spoke sternly. "The article said you guys loved playing ball. It said you were dreaming of the NBA. That's a tough road, boys. Every player that passes through these doors has had a coach he didn't like. Did they quit? No."

I wanted to say something. "Mr. Williams, the NBA is a dream of mine but—"

"But nothing!" Lamar stopped me short, pointing his finger. "You go back and apologize to Coach

Harris. You think I always got along with him when he was my Coach?" He placed his hand on my shoulder and asked me a question that changed my life: "Every dream has a price. Are you willing to pay? Think about it."

CHAPTER FIVE

SKIPPIN' OUT

It was a clear night in New York City. I even managed to see some stars in between tall buildings. I heard a car screech a few blocks away. Someone was blasting their radio in the distance. A woman on a cell phone argued with a friend. The Harlem streets were wide awake. My brother could stay out all night if he wanted to, but I was going home. Tomorrow was a big day.

Ten minutes into my walk, I saw a familiar face on a nearby bench. Cheryl Phelps, a friend from school, waved. "Tony, what are you doing here?" She motioned with her hand. "Sit down."

She was a tiny girl with dark brown skin and curly hair. I sat next to her. Cheryl threw a couple of crumbs from a bag of bread she'd brought to feed some pigeons. "Why are you so quiet?" She asked after awhile.

I grabbed a piece of bread, tossing a few crumbs. "No reason. I'm leaving tomorrow and everything."

Cheryl nodded. "Where's Mike?"

"He went to that party."

"Oh." She paused. "With who?"

"Nick and Devon, why?" I asked.

Her expression changed. "I heard Trevor Samuels was out to get Devon. You should get your brother. Those guys are serious trouble."

My heart started racing. "Where's the party Cheryl?

"Over on 153rd Street. In that old warehouse on the corner."

"I gotta go." I jumped up from the bench and started running...

"Run Hope, run!" Coach Harris was always screaming at me, and last practice of my Sophomore season was no different. "I didn't let you back on this team so you could jog!" Coach constantly reminded me of my freshman mistake.

My ten assists per game that year proved to Coach that I was more than a playground player. But our Sophomore year didn't end in playoff glory. We lost in the opening round to Douglass High. The good news was that my big season had me looking toward a bright future. Mike and I had our sights set on attending the University of New York, like "Sweet Feet."

I spent the summer before my junior year washing cars at Soapy Sid's. This time, I had a partner. Mike and I worked the morning shift together. Then we'd dry our hands for afternoons at the Jungle. Summer came and went the way summertime always does. Those twelve weeks felt more like twelve days. Before I realized what had happened, I was back in school for my junior year.

Something clicked with our team that year. My strong junior season was backed by three post-season wins. Brooklyn Central High was all that stood between us and a state championship. To beat them, we'd have to outplay "Brooklyn's Backcourt," James Thomas and Walter Randolph. This would prove that Mike and I were the two best guards in the city.

Two days prior to the championship game, I walked into the cafeteria feeling good. I was halfway through my lunch by the time the guys got there. I tried to eat fast enough so that I'd have a few minutes to shoot around before sixth period. After all, the biggest game of my life was just around the corner.

Lunchtime in high school was always fun. For fifty minutes, science books and calculators were put aside. We sat in the back row, the basketball table. There weren't assigned seats, but everyone knew where to go. Mike sat to my left and Jermaine Smith was across from me. 'Smitty's' mom would make his lunch every day. Watching him eat a tuna fish and pickle sandwich was the grossest thing in the world.

Never mind the smell. Dizzy was always on my right, and the rest of the team scattered around Mike.

I finished my lunch and stood up to toss my tray out. Mike pushed down on my shoulders. "Forget to say hello to your brother?" He sat down, biting into his burger.

Dizzy sat down too. "T, did you understand what Mrs. Nelson was talking about in chemistry?" He took a bite of his burger and spit it back out. "I think mine went bad."

Mike grabbed the burger from Dizzy and ate the rest of it. "I think they're great." Mike would eat anything.

Chemistry was one of my favorite subjects. I was always explaining stuff to Dizzy. "She was talking about neutrons and electrons. Those little particles that—" Dizzy stopped listening. He was staring at a table of girls. I stopped talking and stared along with him.

Smitty unwrapped his tuna and pickle sandwich. I stood up to leave as he took his first bite. He mashed food in his mouth as he spoke. "Wherg er yer gering?"

"What?" Dizzy, Mike, and I all asked at once.

Smitty swallowed. "Where are you going?"

The guys were looking at me. "To shoot around in the gym." I answered.

Dizzy rolled his eyes. Smitty picked a piece of pickle off the table and ate it. Mike patted my back. "If practice made perfect, you'd never miss a shot,

T."

Just as I was about to walk away, Samantha Lewis approached our table. Dizzy tried to look cool. "What's up?" His voice cracked.

Samantha leaned over the table, speaking to Mike. "You guys want to skip out on school for the rest of the day and go to the zoo?"

We all looked at one another with wide eyes. Samantha was hot! Mike answered for all of us. "Absolutely."

She smiled. "Great. Meet us out front in fifteen minutes."

She left the table. Rick Haynes, our power forward, spoke from a few seats down. "Where are we going?"

Mike was the captain of the team, the pilot. When he spoke, everyone followed his directions. We all had a hard time telling him no. He passed through life like he had everything figured out. But he never understood that some risks weren't worth taking. I took him aside. "This is stupid, Mike. We've got the state championship game in two days. If you get caught, they won't let you play."

He stood up, smiling at the table. "Well boys," I was sure I had talked some sense into him, "let's not get caught." He winked at me. As usual, Mike wasn't going to change his mind.

"If Coach finds out, you guys are in serious trouble." I said.

Paul Miller, our center and the biggest guy in school, agreed. "Yeah, I'm not going either. Can't risk it."

Mike smiled. "I think Samantha likes you, Paul. She was staring right at you."

Paul looked over at me. "Sorry T, I gotta go."

I shook my head. "I'm going to shoot around. Practice starts in four hours."

Mike slapped me five. "Work on those threes! We're gonna need to light up the board against Brooklyn Central." He left the cafeteria. Dizzy, Paul, Rick, and Jermaine followed.

Practice started at three o'clock that afternoon. I was there at two, right after the bell rang. Guys trickled in every few minutes. They changed, and came out to shoot before Coach showed up. Mike still hadn't arrived at 2:57. The door to the gym was open, giving me a view of the front door to the school. If Mike made it back from the zoo, this was his only way in.

The clock struck 3:01. Coach Harris was also late. My brother must have been the luckiest person in the world. This was the first time Coach had missed the start of practice during my two years on the team.

I shot three pointers from the left corner of the court. This was where I had the best view of the front door. It opened and closed twice, but no Mike. "Hello gentlemen." Coach Harris's voice rang out. He looked at the clock on the wall, 3:05. "Sorry I'm late." Everyone was at practice with the exception of Mike, Dizzy,

Paul, Jermaine, and Rick. Coach realized we were missing guys immediately. "Where's your brother, Tony?"

I paused. I didn't know what to say. Then I watched the front door to the school open over Coach's left shoulder. Mike gave me a look and darted toward the back door to the locker room. The guys followed. Coach repeated himself. "Where is your brother? And where's Dizzy and Rick? Paul and Jermaine? What's going on?"

I didn't want to lie to Coach. But the guys had arrived. If I could just stall him for a second, everything would be fine. "Um, I think they're changing."

Coach threw me a curve. "I've got to go talk to them." He started walking toward the locker room.

I jumped in front of Coach. The team must have thought I'd gone crazy. Coach looked puzzled. "Tony, what are you doing?"

I wasn't sure. "When we run our zone defense am I supposed to drop down if they pass to the post?" I hoped this question would buy Mike and the guys some time.

Coach walked to the free throw line. "If their guard passes inside, you can drop down. But you've got to keep an eye on those guards outside." He stood in a defensive stance. "You lose track of them, they'll rain threes on us all day." He paused. "OK?"

I understood our defense perfectly. I nodded my head.

Coach walked back toward the locker room. I

was panicked. Just as Coach was about to open the door, it opened in front of him. Mike, Dizzy, Jermaine, Paul, and Rick stumbled out. They were lacing up their sneakers and tucking in their practice jerseys.

Coach glared at them suspiciously. "Glad you could make it. Let's get to work."

That practice was exhausting. We spent most of the two and a half hours running up and down the court. When the whistle blew at five thirty, we went to the showers.

"Tony." Coach called out to me before I stepped into the locker room. "Can I see you in my office?"

My heart raced. Coach knew I wasn't confused about our zone defense. He knew I was stalling for Mike and the guys. This was the same man who'd kicked me off the team two years earlier. I was sure I'd fallen onto his bad side again.

I sat down across from Coach. "Tony, I know what you did today." I put my hands over my head. He *did* know. "Your brother, Jermaine, Rick, Paul, and Dizzy are not going to play in the state championships. I know they left school today. Principal Moscati told me they'd all be suspended. That's why I was late. I'm disappointed with your brother." He paused. "But that's not what I want to talk to you about. What you did today was brave. Your heart was in the right place. I don't know if you would have done that two years ago."

Coach was proud of me, but I was devastated. We'd worked so hard to get to the state championship game. With Mike out, I didn't know what to do. I'd never played without my wingman.

We ended up getting humiliated against Brooklyn Central. We lost the game, the state championship, and the title of the best pair of guards in the city. When the buzzer sounded, we'd scored thirty fewer points than our opponent. James Thomas outplayed me all night. He had something to say. "Hey Hope, I thought you were gonna give us a game." Thomas waved at Mike, who sat on the bench in jeans. "You're not much without your brother."

After the game, Mike made me a promise: "I'll never leave you alone out there again."

CHAPTER SIX

FORTY-FOUR

I had to stop my brother before he got to that party. I sprinted toward the warehouse. I noticed a bunch of people running from the building. What was happening? My eyes were looking everywhere, searching for my brother. I stepped over the cracked sidewalk leading to the building—"Bang! Bang! Bang!" The loudest noise I'd ever heard rang out. I fell to the floor, covering my head. "Bang! Bang!" I heard the noise again. Each time the noise exploded my body jolted. A few more teenagers dropped to the floor around me. "Bang! Bang!" A woman screamed. "Somebody's shooting!"

I stood up from the sidewalk and heard sirens in the distance. "Mike!" I yelled into the night. I bolted toward the warehouse as people poured out onto the street. I searched everywhere for Mike...

I scanned through the crowd for my brother. We'd left the apartment for a day at the Jungle, but somehow we'd been separated. It was the fourth of July, and a parade was marching through Harlem. A band pounded their drums. People lined the streets, waving American flags and cheering.

I couldn't find him. I figured he was already at the Jungle. We did everything but sleep down there during the summer before our senior season. We were on a mission to win the state championship.

In years past, we'd watch the parade from Dizzy's balcony, slurping on ice cream cones in the heat. But this summer, I didn't have time for ice cream. I waved to Dizzy and the guys, who were pointing at the band and laughing. I didn't know what was so funny. I leaned on the tips of my toes to get a view over the wall of people. Mike was dribbling through the band, testing his skills and being a clown. He made a nice spin move on a tuba player. I began laughing hysterically. Finally, Mike came across the street. "Those tuba players can't cover me." He laughed and we made our way to the courts. We had a lot of practicing to do.

By the time our senior season rolled around, we were sure we'd get the state title. We entered the playoffs as the number two seed and cruised to the championship game. On the other side of the bracket, top-seeded Brooklyn Central had also made it. This set up Brooklyn's Backcourt versus Harlem's Hope.

And this time, Mike would be in uniform.

Two days before tip-off, the head coach for UNY, added fuel to the fire. "I'm very interested in the state championship game this year. The four guards that are involved are great players. We'll see which pair's better this Thursday. Then we'll try and put'em in an UNY uniform."

Game day arrived. We got off the bus on game night and were hounded by reporters. A pair of old headphones covered my ears as I made my way through the traffic. I knew what was at stake tonight: A state championship and a college scholarship.

I moved to the center of the locker room, beneath the lights that flickered and buzzed. Everyone gathered around me. Pressed in tightly, we all began jumping. I grabbed a pile of hands and shouted. "Who are we?"

"Forty-four! Forty-four!" The guys shouted the number of our school.

"From where?" I screamed, hopping up and down.

"Harlem! Harlem!" The guys yelled.

"*Who* are we?" I screamed even louder.

The volume grew. "Forty-four! Forty-four!"

Coach Harris put his hands in the pile and began jumping up and down with us. "How we gonna get this done tonight?" he shouted.

The answer came loud and proud. "Together!" When we ran out of that locker room, we were together in every sense of the word.

I looked around during warm-ups. A crowd of over 3,500 fans was packed into Tinsley College arena. The stands looked like an overflowing bag of popcorn. I noticed that UNY's Coach Collier was sitting in a front row seat, sipping on an orange soda.

On my first trip up the floor, James Thomas reminded me of why I disliked him. He picked his trash talk up where he left off a year ago. "I know why they call you two the Hope brothers. Cause all you do is *hope* you don't have to play us." He smiled. "Your worst nightmare's coming true tonight."

I winked at Thomas. "Let's do this." I proceeded to cross him up, and dart past him. My explosiveness caught him off guard. When I made my way into the lane Walter Randolph cut in front. His foul sent me falling backward. I lofted a shot that kissed off the glass and dropped in. My free throw completed the three-point play. I was fired up.

I had a feeling that Thomas would try to do something to answer my three-point play. He glared at me near half court, dribbling casually. Suddenly, he charged. I shuffled back, but he stopped on a dime. He thought he had enough separation for a shot. Last year, he probably would have. He squared his shoulders, ready to launch his jumper. But I sprouted into the air like a kangaroo. From three inches above him, I swatted his shot. My block sent the basketball toward the other end of the court.

I sprinted after it, but had to hurry before it rolled out of bounds. As I went airborne, I noticed a figure from the corner of my eye. "On your wing," Mike shouted. I beat Thomas to the ball and slapped it over my left shoulder. From the floor I saw Mike grab the pass and rise up. His dunk put us up 5-0.

We continued the hot start, harassing Brooklyn's Backcourt with defensive pressure. With three minutes left until halftime, we led 44–29. That's when Randolph caught fire. On Brooklyn Central's next four possessions he drained three-pointers. He swished two straight away. His third shot was good from the corner. His last one rattled in from ten feet beyond the arc as the halftime buzzer sounded. Our lead was only three points after some miraculous shooting.

The third quarter was a defensive struggle from the start. Mike and I shadowed Thomas and Randolph. Their shots clanked off the rim and the backboard. Yet, at the close of the third, we led by only five. Coach Harris demanded that we speed up the game's offensive tempo. On our first possession of the fourth Mike took his words to heart. He raced down the court with no regard for his body. He slid between defenders and rose toward the rim. At that same moment, Walter Randolph bumped him from behind. Mike dropped to the floor as the whistle blew. He clutched his knee in pain.

Our trainer helped my brother to the bench, wrapping his knee in ice. I'd seen that expression on

Mike's face before. I was sure I'd be finishing this game without him.

After Mike's injury, Brooklyn rattled off thirteen points. With five minutes left in our season, we trailed by eight. Coach Harris called a time-out. We formed a semicircle around him. "Tony, you've got to start looking inside. And Dizzy, shoot the ball when you're open, son! With Mike out we need—"

"I'm right here Coach." Mike stood up, pulling the ice pack from his purple knee. "I'm ready to play."

Coach put his hands on my brother's shoulders. "Are you sure?"

"I'm not gonna sit here while we blow our last chance. Let's turn this thing around."

We all breathed a sigh of relief and Dizzy found his seat on the bench. Mike was back. I walked onto the floor with my brother half-limping next to me. Thomas looked over at Mike and smiled. "That leg better be working, Hope." Mike didn't say anything.

He walked over to me and whispered, "Feed me the ball, T. We're not losing this game."

Mike dragged his leg forward and pushed up the floor. When I reached half court, I bounced a pass to his side. He caught it awkwardly. Nearly losing his balance, he shot from one leg. The awkward three-pointer tickled nothing but nylon, cutting the lead to five. Mike urged on the crowd with a pump of his fist. Suddenly his limp was more of a strut. And as James Thomas dribbled up the court, the fans were chanting, "Forty-Four."

Thomas tossed a pass over to Randolph, who dribbled left. Mike was waiting for him. He slapped the ball away. I took off with Thomas blanketing me. Mike saw me break and lofted a balloon pass down court. The rainbow had every eye in the house staring toward the rafters. My head bobbed up and down as I sprinted toward the pass. Both my arms stretched and the ball landed softly in my hands. Wearing Thomas like a backpack I rose into the air for a slam. I looked down at him from the rim. "Didn't know I could fly, did you?"

From there, my brother and his dark purple knee took over. If anyone had questioned who the best player on that court was, Mike gave them the answer. He made his next eight shots to keep *Hope* alive. With thirty seconds left we trailed by one.

I dribbled the ball patiently as the clock clicked to twenty-five seconds. "One shot!" Coach Harris screamed from the sidelines. I watched the clock, devising a game plan in my head. "Eighteen seconds, Tony. Stay calm. Careful with the ball. Don't show'em where you're going. Find Mike. There he is. He's covered. Get open, Mike. Fifteen seconds. Come on Mike, get open. Thirteen seconds. Here comes Thomas, he'll try for the steal. Twelve...Eleven! Now go!"

Randolph had Mike wrapped up like a birthday present. I checked out my other options. Jermaine Smith was covered. Rick Haynes tried to fight through a pick. No one had an inch.

With seven seconds remaining I looked toward the hoop. The final shot would be mine. I faked left, then crossed over right. Thomas lost a half step. I had a lane! Will Bromwell came charging at me with his arms raised high. Four seconds. Fading back, I chucked one up. I thought my shot had a chance. But the ball ricocheted off the rim and into the air. I'd missed the game winner. Their giant center positioned himself in front of the basket. Three seconds left. Hands grabbed for the ball. It hung in the air forever. Two seconds. From nowhere, I saw my brother flying toward the pile of hands. His extended left arm hovered above the rim. He barely reached the ball as the clock wound down to one.

I don't understand how he did it. But his banged up knee shot him six feet through the air and above the pile beneath the basket. His arm powered the ball through the defenders and through the net before the buzzer sounded. He fell to the floor with the ball bouncing next to him. We'd won the state championship!

For twelve guys and Coach Harris, there was no greater sight in the world than my brother's dunk. We mobbed the court as champions.

Three days later Coach Collier called, offering two full scholarships to attend the University of New York. Mike and I accepted. Coach gave us some advice: "Stay in shape and out of trouble this summer."

I only wish that Mike had listened.

CHAPTER SEVEN

INVINCIBLE

The night my life changed was exactly three months after winning the state championship—less than fifteen hours before we were supposed to leave for UNY. We'd played our last game at the Jungle earlier.

I followed Mike all over Harlem that night. I watched him hide behind dumpsters to avoid the police. I watched him pass "Sweet Feet's" house without a second glance. Finally, I stood in front of the warehouse, where I heard gunshots.

Nick and Devon sprinted past me on my way to the entrance. They were both holding guns. Sirens sounded. "Where's Mike?" I screamed. Running like cowards, they didn't answer. They sprinted toward the alley. Two police officers trailed close behind them.

The front window to the warehouse had been

sprayed with bullets. I stepped over broken glass as I moved closer to the door. The sounds of sirens grew louder. I waited for Mike to follow his friends out. "Mike!" I shouted. "Mike!"

Another police car arrived. I watched as Devon was pushed into the backseat of the car in handcuffs. He and Nick had been caught. Tears rolled down Nick's cheeks as he spoke to me. "I'm sorry, T. Mike didn't want this." He looked at the warehouse.

Right then, I knew where Mike was. I ran past two policemen. My right hand pushed the door open. When I looked down, I saw a face that looked like my own. "Oh my God! Mike!" I screamed. I was standing over my brother. He'd been shot.

Mike lay still on the floor, barely conscious. "C'mon Mike," I squeezed his hand, feeling nothing in return. "Let's go, Hope, fight! Fight, Mike!"

An instant later, paramedics were pushing me out of the way and placing Mike onto a stretcher. They stuck him with needles and gave him oxygen. Before I knew it, the ambulance was speeding away toward the hospital with both of us inside.

Mike was tied to machines I'd only seen in the movies. Something was in his mouth and towels were wrapped tightly around his wounds. I shuffled behind him and reached down to grab his hand. "I'm right here bro—still right here. Don't leave, I need you. Fight, Mike!" His eyes moved around in circles like he was looking for something. Finally, they found mine. "I need you," I whispered.

I looked over at the screen monitoring his barely beating heart. I squeezed his hand tighter. What if Mike died? How could I go on without my wingman? The next morning we were supposed to leave for UNY. Just as we pulled up to the emergency room Mike surprised everyone with a huge gasp for air. He wasn't giving up. The doors of the ambulance opened and Mike was rolled out like a tornado. In a flash, he was moved into a room I wasn't allowed to enter.

On the other side of that door my brother fought for his life. Our dreams were suddenly unimportant. All that mattered was Mike staying alive. By being at that party he'd made the worst mistake of his life. I realized that I had as well—I should have stopped him.

I was crying in a dark green chair when I heard Mom's voice. "Tony, what happened?" She was hysterical. I'd never seen Mom cry like she did that night. She hugged me and spoke through tears. "Why did my baby get shot?"

Mom sat down. I stopped crying. I didn't want to tell Mom what happened. She'd worked so hard to keep us out of trouble. The only thing that kept our family together was the strength of our mother. If she lost Mike tonight, I wondered if she'd ever be strong again. "Tell me he's gonna be okay, Tony."

I wasn't sure if I believed it, but I knew something had to be said. "He's gonna be fine, Mom. I know it. He took a deep breath as we came into the hospital. He'll be okay."

Mom was trying to calm herself. "Where did he get shot?"

I couldn't look at her. "In the back. I guess Nick and Devon had some enemies at the party they went to. They started shooting. Nick and Devon shot back. Mike was running away, and he got hit—" Tears rolled down my face. "He got shot three times, Mom." Neither one of us said much after that.

I sat on the floor while Mom stared at the wall blankly, squeezing my hand every so often. Five hours passed. The waiting was unbearable. At any moment, doctors would tell me if my brother was dead or alive.

Mom had always told us how precious life was. In the time it takes to cough, sneeze, flinch, burp, step, or smile—poof—it can all be over. A night of partying with the wrong crowd can turn into disaster. Life is a delicate egg, and if you treat it any other way, you'll end up scrambled.

Suddenly, the door to Mike's room swung open. Mom and I leaped to our feet. We walked toward a black doctor in her early thirties. She had a strange expression on her face. I tried to read it, but couldn't. She approached us and removed her mask. "Mike is alive and in stable condition."

I hugged my mother. "My baby's okay. He's okay." Mom repeated this again and again. Mike

Hope had stayed alive.

After hugging Mom for a moment I looked over my shoulder. The doctor was still standing there. She had something else to say. My sense of relief was put on hold. I looked at her anxiously. "Is my brother OK?"

She cleared her throat. "It was a miracle that Mike survived. He took three bullets in the back from close range." The doctor was rattled. "Two of the bullets that entered Mike's back missed his vital organs by centimeters. That's the only reason he's still alive. But the third bullet—" She took a deep breath. "The third bullet hit Mike in his spinal chord. We did all we could. I'm sorry, but Mike's paralyzed from the waist down."

Right in the middle of the word "paralyzed," Mom dropped to the floor. She wasn't crying anymore, she was numb. The doctor continued. "He needs to rest for a few hours before you can see him. I'm sorry."

I helped Mom into a chair. Meanwhile, I was pacing around the room. "Paralyzed from the waist down." I kept replaying those words in my head. "Paralyzed from the waist down." After everything we'd been through together—all the training, all the dreaming, UNY, NBA plans, it all came down to those words. "Paralyzed from the waist down."

Suddenly, I couldn't stop crying. My best friend, my shadow, would never walk again. Basket-

ball had been taken away from Mike Hope. Nobody loved the game like my brother.

After hours of waiting, a nurse told us that Mike was ready for visitors. "Mom, you go ahead. I'll go after." She kissed me on the head and walked into the room. I sat back down on the floor. I didn't know what I would say to my brother.

I closed my eyes and was on a hardwood floor in a New York Pride jersey. Two defenders darted toward me. I picked up my dribble and threw a pass that Mike caught in stride. I watched him soar to the hoop and hammer home a dunk.

When I opened my eyes, I didn't hear the screams of excited fans. I was still in the hospital waiting room. My brother was paralyzed. The sounds of Mom crying shook the hallways.

About twenty minutes later, Mom went to a nearby room to lie down. She was exhausted. A freckled nurse waved me in. "Your brother's been asking for you." I stood up from my seat. When I entered the room Mike was staring out the window. He was lying on his back perfectly still. I wondered what he was thinking. When I was a few feet away he turned his head toward me. "Where you been? Scared to see me?" Mike knew me better than I knew myself.

I spoke softly. "No, I just wanted to give Mom a chance—you know. How are you?"

"I got shot in the back three times, Tony. I'm not doing that well."

I'd thought about what I would say to my brother for the past three hours. But all I came up with was a stupid question. "Does it hurt?"

Mike's eyes welled up with tears. He looked scared. "I don't know, T, I can't feel anything."

I burst into tears. "What did you do, Mike?" I yelled at him. "What did you do to yourself?" I cried on his shirt. His hands palmed over the top of my head.

"Easy, T. I'm all right. I'm still talking to you, aren't I? I'm not dead. I'm still here." I had to get control of myself. I pulled up a seat next to him. He spoke in a serious tone. "I'm done with basketball. I'm done with walking to the store, even standing up. I know this. But I still feel lucky. I should be dead." He paused. "Do you know why I'm alive?" I shook my head and Mike continued, "Because you need me. That's what you told me when I was in the ambulance. That's what I kept telling myself. That's why I kept fighting."

Mike moved his head around on the bed. He was searching for a comfortable spot. I sensed his frustration and propped up his pillow. "Thanks." He wasn't finished yet. "Tony, you're Harlem's Hope now. You're my hope. You've got to take us to the top. Just like we planned."

I know he wanted me to tell him I was ready to take on life without him but I wasn't. "It shouldn't have happened like this. It was supposed to be you *and me. How am I supposed to play without you?" I laid my head back down on Mike's stomach.*

"Tony. Look at me, this is important." I picked my head up. "You're gonna be a star." He cleared his throat. "Someday you're gonna have a moment where everything will become clear for you. And you'll realize—you've always been great."

I put my head back on his chest. I was sure that day would never come. Mike wanted me to continue our dream. But sitting there in that room, nothing seemed important anymore.

CHAPTER EIGHT

THE FARMER

The morning Mike came home from the hospital we had pancakes. Mom and I sat around the kitchen table as Mike wheeled himself over. His chair banged into the table as he tried to adjust his position. He could barely reach his plate. Mom looked over at me. "Tony, help your brother."

Mike bumped the table again. I started to stand, but Mike didn't want my help. "Sit down, T. I can do this. You have to let me do this stuff." Mom and I tried not to stare at Mike. It was hard. He bumped the table again, this time his fork dropped to the floor. I started to stand. "Tony, sit down! I'll use my spoon."

I stared at the fork lying on the floor. I didn't know how to act. Everything inside me wanted to help. Instead, I grabbed a pancake and dropped it onto my plate. A strange silence took over the room. The only noise we could hear was the creaking of Mike's chair. From the corner of my eye, I glanced at him. Sweat beads dripped off his forehead. Our eyes met and I glanced back at my pancakes.

It's a strange thing being twin brothers. You grow to be an extension of one another. That's why in those moments I felt like I knew what Mike was feeling. I stared at my food, unable to eat. Mike reached forward, but couldn't get to his food. Finally, he gave up, tossing his spoon and rolling himself into the living room.

Mom looked over at me. I didn't know what to say. Mike broke the silence from the other room. "Tony, what are you still doing here? You were supposed to leave for school two weeks ago. If you want to help me, go to college. You've gotta give me time to get used to this." If Mike could still move his legs, I was sure he would have pushed me out the door. As he was, he just stared at me.

The truth was, I was scared of facing life without Mike. Still, I boarded the train and left Harlem that night. An hour later, I lugged a green duffle bag through Van Patten Hall, my college dormitory and strange new home. My bag dragged on the dirty floor. A kid on a skateboard hopped over it as he passed. Loud music rattled the walls. The sounds were different than the sounds I'd grown up with. The people seemed different too.

I unlocked the door to Room 18, a small place

with plain furniture. Inside, there was two of every-thing. Two beds, two desks, two chairs, and two lamps on opposite sides of the room. I dropped my bag onto the left bed and stared at the walls. The bed across from me was covered with CDs I'd never heard of.

The door swung open a moment later. A tall, thin, goofy-looking white guy stumbled into the room. He extended his hand. "Are you Tony?"

I shook his hand. "Yeah, I'm Tony."

"I'm Josh, Josh Gibson. My friends call me Gibby. I guess we're roommates. I've got allergies so I took the bed away from the window. Is that cool?"

My head nodded. I was barely listening to what Josh was saying.

He tried to make conversation. "So, you run the point? I play two guard." He paused. "I'm not Mike but—"

"These rooms are tiny." I changed the subject, unwilling to discuss my brother. Mike was headline news in New York. Everyone had a comment about him. I turned my back to Josh and began unpacking. I'd never shared a room with anyone besides Mike. And this Josh guy was annoying. We had nothing in common. He was from some farm in Pennsylvania. I was from Harlem. What did I know about a farm? This was gonna be a long year. We weren't going to be friends. "Listen Gibson, you keep yourself on that side of the room and we'll be alright." Our conversation was over.

When I went to bed that night I wondered if I'd made a mistake coming to UNY. Josh interrupted my thoughts. He whispered from across the dark room. "Tony, you awake?" I pretended to be asleep. He continued anyway. "I know I'm a farm boy and you're from the city, but I'd like to be friends."

I didn't want to make friends. I wanted my brother. He should have been lying in that bed, not some farmer. I remained silent. A moment later, I closed my eyes and went to sleep.

Basketball practice the next morning was awful. After warm-ups and a short meeting, the freshmen scrimmaged against last year's starters. Josh played on my team along with three other newcomers. Surprisingly, Gibson was a solid player. His goofiness masked athleticism and a sweet jump shot. I couldn't help imagining how good our freshman class would have been with Mike.

I was completely out of it during that scrimmage. I turned the ball over again and again. With the upperclassmen leading by four, I dribbled into the front court. There was one defender in front of me. I felt another closing in from my left. "On your wing, T. On your wing if you need me." I heard Mike's voice and threw a perfect pass to my right. The ball bounced twice on the hardwood floor before sailing out of bounds. No one was there.

Coach Collier's southern accent rang out. "Hey Hope! Are you with us?" I didn't answer, staring at the sidelines, dazed. "Hallaway, run the point! Hope, take a breather."

I walked over to the bench. Coach Collier came over and sat next to me. I looked him in the eyes as he spoke. "You've gotta screw your head on straight, Hope. This team needs you. You've got to find your game out there." He patted me on the back. "Come back in when you're ready, Tony." I never returned to the floor that day.

The first few weeks of school were terrible. I barely spoke to Gibson. And I wasn't having fun playing ball. Wherever I went, I heard the sounds of Harlem in my head. I began to wonder why I left.

One Thursday, after a bad test grade, I decided enough was enough. Nothing was going my way at UNY. The time had come to go home. Class let out and I jogged back to the dorm to pack my stuff. As I turned the key to enter my room loud music blared from inside. It was *my* music. Josh was sitting on the edge of my bed, bouncing to the beat. He was looking through my CD case. He didn't hear the door open when I came in.

All the emotions running through my body erupted. I grabbed Josh by the shirt. "What did I tell you, Gibson? What did I say about my stuff?" Josh looked scared. "Answer me, Gibson! Didn't I tell you to keep off my stuff?"

He pushed my hand away from his shirt and looked the other way. "You're crazy, Hope. You know that?" He paused. "You haven't even tried with me since the moment I got here."

"Tried what?" I said.

"Did you ever try to give me a chance? The answer's no." Josh tossed my CD case onto my bed. "Keep your CDs."

Josh's comment got to me. I sat down. "The only reason I'm here is because UNY wanted my brother. He was the best player in the country last year. We were a package deal." I paused. "But he got shot. Now he can't walk." I wasn't sure I could finish my sentence. "I'm sorry for not giving you a chance, I just miss playing ball with Mike."

The expression on Josh's face changed. "I know about your brother, T. I'm sorry."

There was more I had to say. "This room was supposed to be for Mike and me. This was supposed to be our dream. That dream's over. I'm leaving here tonight." I began emptying my drawers into my bag.

After I had filled the bag halfway, Josh turned it upside down. T-shirts and socks tumbled to the floor. "I can't let you leave, Tony. I've spent my whole life trying to get here. You have too. I can't let you throw that away. If your brother was here he'd tell you the same thing."

My mind was made up. "You're not my brother. I'm leaving." I began repacking.

Gibson tumbled my bag upside down again. "You don't understand. I'm going to play in the NBA.

And if you leave, that might not happen."

"Me and you have nothing to do with one another, Gibson." I pushed Josh aside. "Now move."

He bounced back into place. "You and I are the best players in the freshman class. Without you, it's just me. You know what that means? When I'm a senior, the NBA scouts won't look my way because UNY won't be a team to look at." Josh pleaded with me. "You're a great point guard. And I can score. Maybe not the way your brother could, but I made it here for a reason too. Just give me a chance." Josh spoke with so much feeling in his voice, he reminded me of Mike. "Let's go down to the courts, the lights are on until ten."

I started to smile. "You wanna be my wingman, farmer? You better be good." I dropped my duffle bag and laced up my high-tops.

We walked down to the courts together. Josh bounced the ball the entire way. He talked about life on the farm. He used to wake up at sunrise and shoot baskets on a hoop in the middle of some cornfields. I told him that I'd never even seen cornfields.

Then he started talking about life without a dad. His Mom worked two jobs to pay the bills. His story about growing up with a single Mom sounded just like mine. He spoke and I found myself finishing his sentences. We had more in common than I thought.

By the time we were a block from the court, I was telling Josh all about basketball in Harlem. He couldn't believe my stories. "You guys play five-on-five every day? Back home, I can't even find someone to rebound for me."

When we reached the court we saw two familiar faces. Billy Cunningham and Jason Jackson were playing a night game of H-O-R-S-E. They were the senior guards on our team. These were the same guys Josh and I would be backing up. Immediately, Josh challenged them to a game of two-on-two. Billy and Jason wanted to split the teams up, "making it fair," as Cunningham said in a cocky voice. We insisted on playing young guys versus old.

Although we were juiced, Cunningham and Jackson were half-asleep. The game started. While dribbling, Cunningham told Jackson about some girl he'd met at a party. Jackson made weak cuts to the basket through fits of laughter. Cunningham's tale continued as he nailed a jumper over me. Then another. Then another—all the while, detailing his story. This guy wasn't taking me seriously.

I hadn't proven myself at UNY. Now I was being embarrassed. Cunningham wouldn't shut up. "So then, she tells her friend Holly that—" I was done with his stupid story. I swiped the ball from his hands. At the top of the key I bounced a pass to Josh who nailed a jumper.

I looked over at Cunningham and smiled. "Three-one. Story time over yet?"

Suddenly, I was dribbling intensely. I was also

doing something I hadn't done in the five weeks since Mike's accident. I was having fun on a basketball court.

Cunningham and Jackson never found a flow. On the other hand, Josh and I played well together. We took a surprising fourteen-six lead over the seniors. On game point, I had Cunningham confused. I dribbled forward, then backward, and then behind my back. The senior lunged for the ball. Jackson saw a chance at a steal and came over to apply the double team. Instinctively, I threw the ball toward the rim. When trapped, I'd always toss it up toward the rim. And I'd always have Mike there to grab it and score. But with Mike in Harlem, I was sure I'd turned the ball over. I watched my pass float to the hoop and toward the out of bounds line.

Without my brother, things would never be the same on a basketball court. Bad passes around the rim would no longer be assists. I began wondering again, *Was I really a playmaker or had Mike just made great plays?*

This thought was erased as Gibby rose up from the baseline. In mid-air, he caught the ball and slammed it home. I raised my arms in triumph. I was a playmaker, and the farmer could play.

CHAPTER NINE

STEPPING INTO THE LIGHT

Mom didn't raise quitters, I stayed at UNY.

My freshman season began a week after our two-on-two game. We began against Rhode Island State's Flying Fish, an unranked team. We entered the game as the seventh-ranked team in the nation. We fully expected a blowout. Yet somehow, the Fish hung around. With ten minutes remaining in the second half, they trailed by four.

Cunningham ran the point during those first thirty minutes. Even the best-conditioned point guard had trouble playing without a break. I noticed him gasping for air and glanced over at Coach Collier. Coach ran his fingers through his thinning hair. "Hope, get in there for Cunningham."

I tore off my warm-ups on my way to the scorer's table. From the moment I stepped onto the court, I noticed something different about college basketball. The game at the Division I level was played at a frantic pace. If you blinked, you were beaten.

I dribbled to half court and passed the ball over to Vance Wilson. My pass was tipped and stolen. The defender went coast to coast for an easy lay-up.

Clinging to a two-point lead, Coach Collier signaled for a timeout. Right away, he looked over at Cunningham. "You ready, Billy?"

After one trip down the floor, Cunningham was back in the game and I was back on the bench. That turnover was the first of many in an ugly second half. The final score was Rhode Island State 86, UNY 78. Our season had opened disastrously. And a tough road trip was coming.

The first of these games was against the University of Trenton Pit Bulls. They were ranked thirteenth in the nation. Playing in front of their fans was difficult. The Kennel, as it was called, was one of the loudest arenas in college basketball. UNY had lost the last three times they played in Trenton.

When I entered the gym for warm-ups, I was overwhelmed. Cameras shot from every angle. Television announcers combed their hair and reviewed statistics. Cheerleaders flipped and coaches paced. Then there was the crowd. At Trenton, twenty thousand screaming fans packed the Kennel. They chewed on dog bones, barked, and howled. It was madness.

When warm-ups ended I found my seat. I hated

my view from the bench.

The Pit Bulls dominated the first half. Their defense limited our clean looks at the basket. We couldn't get anything going and trailed by eleven, 45-34 at the break.

Halftime hardly cooled the Pit Bulls. Their seven-foot center, Steve House, hit his first four shots after intermission. His eight points made their advantage nineteen.

When Cunningham went left around a sophomore point guard, things got worse. . The Pit Bull lunged for the ball and poked Cunningham in the eye. The whistle blew and Billy dropped to the floor.

After my miscue against Rhode Island State, I thought C.J. Katz would step in for Cunningham. Coach checked down the bench, searching for something to ignite his squad. "Hope, Gibson, get over here!" When Josh and I stood up, some of the Pit Bull players smirked. They assumed that Coach Collier had given up. In front of a packed house, with the season only a week old, two freshmen stepped into the light.

Coach shouted over the crowd. "OK boys, show us something." Josh and I tapped the top of the scorer's table, checking ourselves into the game. I bent down and touched the number 44 on my sneakers. That was Mike's number.

Vance Wilson passed it in to me. I threw a pass over to Josh, who was hounded by a bigger defender.

Intimidated, he threw it back out to me. I waited for someone to get open. The defense reacted to every glance I shot at my teammates. I dribbled but couldn't find a seam. By the time I tossed another pass to Josh, the shot clock had expired. That was my second turnover in two college possessions.

Coach Collier peered over at Cunningham, who held an ice pack over his eye. Beads of sweat formed on Coach's forehead. He clapped his hands. "Let's go guys. Focus!"

The Pit Bulls' point guard dished to his right after crossing half court. Josh lunged, cutting off the passing lane. He got control of the ball and dribbled down the floor with one defender between himself and the basket. When he reached the free-throw line he stopped short and pulled a jumper. Two points.

We were so excited that we left Andy Fox with a wide open lay-up on the other end. But a stroke of luck spit his shot off the rim and at my chest. I started the break, ball by my side, clear sailing to the basket. But Fox hustled back, jumping into me as I rose to the hoop. His foul knocked both of us to the floor hard. The pain quickly went away when I watched the ball drop into the hoop. And stepping up to the line, I swished a free throw. Trenton's lead was cut to fourteen.

Andy Fox was shaken after his missed lay-up. Our defense applied a full court press and he panicked. He carelessly passed the ball off Steve House's left foot. I picked up the loose ball and fed Josh. His three was perfect. The lead was back down to eleven.

During the next ten minutes we were awesome. Led defensively by Philadelphia's Finest, Leroy Hill, we cut the lead to two. Offensively, Josh and I were raining threes. I even caught Coach pumping his fist.

With three minutes left, I shuffled in front of the Pit Bulls' Jeff Cass. He waved his hands at half court, directing his teammates. I paid attention to his passing lanes, backpedaling to close them off. When he noticed some separation, he stepped up and buried a shot. He was five feet beyond the three-point line. I never saw it coming.

Down by five with a minute-thirty remaining, we faced an important possession. I dribbled quickly. The clock was my enemy, ticking closer to triple zeros. At the three-point line, I tossed up a prayer. With the game on the line, I'd made a bad decision. Unless a gust of wind carried the ball, this one was way short. My shot barely nipped the rim. Luckily, it landed in the largest pair of hands on the floor. Thank goodness for Leroy Hill! He held the rebound above the defense and dropped in a three-foot hook shot.

With fifty-five seconds left, Trenton's Jeff Cass pushed the ball up. I was in his hip pocket like loose change. There was no way he was going to shoot again. Uncomfortable, Cass passed to his back-court mate, Dante Adams. He launched an ugly jumper that smacked iron. Leroy Hill roared as he collected another rebound. He handed me the ball.

I streaked toward the basket. Three points down. Forty-seven seconds left. I leaped into a crowd of players. Two Pit Bull defenders went airborne to block my shot. I wasn't going to float the ball over these trees. Instead, I spun in mid-air, shuffling a pass to Leroy. He worked his magic again, banking in a short hook shot.

Thirty seconds remained as Jeff Cass entered the frontcourt. I fouled him immediately. He made one of his free throws. We trailed by two with twenty-nine seconds left. Coach Collier raised his pointer finger in the air. "One shot. Philadelphia," he demanded. "Philadelphia" was a play we'd practiced for this situation.

Leroy Hill moved into the low block. We were ready. I zipped a pass to Josh in the corner. Fifteen seconds. Gibby secured a passing lane. His bounce pass landed in Leroy's hands. The big man drew a double team. Nine seconds. Leroy pump-faked, but no one budged. The play was broken. He passed the ball back to me at the top of the key. Five seconds. I dribbled twice and bumped Cass to create some space. Two seconds. I jumped backward and released a shot. As I let the ball go, Cass slapped my wrist. The shot rimmed out but the referee noticed the contact. His whistle blew, directing me to the foul line.

With a line of zeros on the clock, I had to make both free throws to force overtime. I stepped to the line for the first. Thousands of faces and waving arms distracted me from behind the backboard. I went through my pre-shot routine. I took three dribbles. I closed my eyes. I pictured the ball dropping through the hoop. Then I took a look at the rim, released and followed through.

My first shot was perfect. I knew it the second I let go, all net.

The referee grabbed the ball. "Timeout, Trenton." They'd purposely called that timeout to upset my rhythm.

I jogged over to the bench. My teammates stood around Coach Collier. "Okay, five minutes of overtime after Tony makes this shot. We win that, then we eat. Burgers or pizza?" Coach's joke relaxed me, if just for the moment.

The whistle blew and I walked to the free throw line. The ref tossed me the ball. Holding the game in my hands, I went through my routine again. "Release, follow through." I repeated this in my head. "Release, follow through."

I released, but didn't follow through. The line drive hit the front of the rim and dropped to the floor. I stood alone as my teammates left the court. We'd come three inches short of overtime. The crowd stood celebrating their team's victory. I felt terrible. I'd let my team down.

Cunningham's eye healed quickly, and I was back on the bench. Although I learned a great deal about the game that season, I was ready to be a star.

Cunningham was nearing graduation. My opportunity was just around the corner.

Our season ended with a first-round loss to Western State in the college championship tournament. Coach Collier snapped a comment my way in the locker room after the game. "Be ready to run the point next season, Hope. You're our guy."

CHAPTER TEN

FROM SCRATCH

I returned to Harlem for the summer. When I arrived home, something occurred to me. Mike had spent close to a year in his wheelchair. I tried to imagine what that must have been like, but couldn't. Our life had been split apart. For the first time, we met new experiences alone. I had just gone through my first year of college basketball. Mike had been living life without his legs.

Mom made Mike's new life easier by rearranging the apartment. Before his injury there was stuff all over the place. But when I came home after that first summer, everything had changed. There was no clutter on the floor, nothing to get caught in Mike's wheels. I watched him move around the apartment with the grace he once walked with. He grabbed my bag from in front of the door, carrying it down the hallway. He was moving with confidence. I followed him into our bedroom, smiling.

"What did you do to this place?" I was staring at our *clean* room.

The beds were made and laundry was in the basket. Even the smell was fresh. Aside from that, our room had turned into a gym. Weights lined the walls in columns. Barbells were in neat rows by the foot of Mike's bed. As for Mike himself, his upper body was huge.

I picked up a weight. "Do you lift these?" I asked, unable to do it myself.

He lifted the weight with ease and did a few curls. "Not bad, huh?"

"Not bad." I glanced around the walls. There were articles pinned everywhere. I leaned in closer. Each article described a miracle. One was the story of a blind man who regained his sight. Another described a kid who'd been in a coma and awoke. The title of the article was, "Miracles Happen All the Time." Mike had circled it. At the center of his display was a story about a woman who'd fully recovered from paralysis. The picture showed her training with weights.

"So this stuff really happens, huh?" I read on about the woman who regained use of her legs. "The doctor said she'd never walk again."

Mike wheeled himself closer to me. "I don't believe in never, T."

I turned toward him. "Where'd you get all these

books?"

"At school. I've been spending a lot of time reading." After Mike's injury, he elected not to attend the University of New York. Life had altered that path. Instead, he attended Harlem College, where he wheeled himself every morning.

"How you doing in school?" I asked. "Second semester go as well as the first?"

Mike smiled. "I got a 4.0. I'm a studious student, T. You wouldn't believe it."

I paused, "Do you want to—"

He spoke through my words. "I don't think so, T."

"Let me ask at least. Do you want to come down to the courts with me?"

Mike shook his head and smiled. "I knew you were going to ask me that."

"We can go down to that hoop over by Dizzy's place. It'll be fun."

"I don't know, T."

I grabbed a basketball from the corner of the room and fired it at Mike. He caught it without flinching. The sound made a pop. Palming the ball in his right hand, he closed his eyes. He moved his upper body like he was about to make a lay-up. He tossed the ball back to me. "I'll watch you shoot." Just holding that ball was enough to convince Mike.

We got there a few minutes later and I began firing away. The basket was set on uneven gravel. There were no nets and the rim bent forward. People rarely shot here. That's why I knew this would be a good place to go. Mike would be uncomfortable with everyone watching him.

While I shot, he collected rebounds, talking about life in Harlem. I tried to describe the speed of college basketball to Mike. I told him about UNY and Gibby too. He'd watched every minute I'd played on television. I mentioned that Coach Collier told me I'd be the starting point guard. He was excited for me.

I bricked one off the rim and Mike went after it. He moved himself over to the ball swiftly. After he tracked it down, he threw a pass toward the basket. I rose up, grabbed the rock, and slammed it through the crooked rim. For a moment, we were playing together again.

I made a few in a row and passed the ball to Mike four feet from the basket. After spinning the leather in his hands, he threw it toward the rim. His shot bounced off the glass and in.

"Nice shot. Try one from farther out." I said.

With some confidence, he rolled to the top of the key. I tossed him the pill. Mike leaned forward and took his shot. It was on line, but came up short, barely touching the front iron. I grabbed the rebound and passed to Mike again. "Try another one."

His expression changed as he passed the ball back to me. "Nah, you go ahead. I'll rebound."

When my brother had his legs to support his

shot, he never hit the front iron. When we left the courts, I tried not to look shaken. Mike wasn't fooled. "I know what you're thinking, T. But I'm happy, Tony." *He* was the one in the wheelchair, cheering *me* up. Mike didn't need basketball anymore.

July turned into August, and, once again, my time in Harlem was over. A week before my sophomore season, I received news that Coach Collier was retiring. Right away, I thought this was a bad break for me. Coach Collier had assured me that I was going to be the starting point guard. What if our new coach had other ideas?

I arrived at the first scheduled practice. Josh greeted me at center court, biting the nails on his shooting hand. "See that guy in the bleachers? I think he's our new coach." There had been no announcement as to who would take over the program. Josh spit a nail onto the court. "Coach Collier told this guy we were starters, right?"

"Of course," I answered, not believing what I said.

In the middle of our conversation I heard a voice. A tall black man hidden in the shadows blew his whistle. "Nobody shoot until we've stretched." The man's face was disguised by dim lighting. Everyone dropped to the floor. We'd just met our new coach.

The mystery man edged closer as we stretched. I tapped Josh on the shoulder. "Is that who I think it is?"

Entranced, Josh spoke. "That's 'Sweet Feet' Williams!"

The legend had traded in his high-tops for a coach's whistle. He strutted to center court. We all stopped stretching. In disbelief, we watched his every move. Lamar Williams was standing in our gym. "I'm Lamar Williams, your new coach." Whispers flooded the gym. Lamar's deep voice grew louder. "You can call me Coach or Coach Williams, whichever you'd like."

Leroy Hill spoke up first. "What about 'Sweet Feet?'"

Coach chuckled along with the rest of us. "Sweet Feet's retired. It's Coach or Coach Williams, okay?" His smile faded. "On this court, my feet aren't moving, yours are." He tried to make eye contact with everyone in the circle. "In the next three weeks, the only thing *sweet* is gonna be when practice ends. I'm gonna work you guys harder than you've ever worked. Before the season ends, I'm gonna teach you what it takes to win. Some of you may think you know how to win." He grabbed my hand, staring at my fingers. He did the same to Josh, then to a couple others. "I don't see any championship rings, though." He pulled a shining gold NBA championship ring off his finger. "I never got one of these in college. I'd like to."

He reached into his right pocket and removed a sheet of paper. "Coach Collier was kind enough to jot down the starting lineup he'd drawn up for the season." I looked over at Josh, relieved. We'd be starting after all. Lamar looked over the paper for a few seconds. "I respect Coach Collier very much, but today we start from scratch." He crumpled the sheet and threw it toward the sideline. "We'll find a lineup that works. For now, start running. I'll tell you when to stop. And if you finish last on my court, you clean up after practice."

Before we ran, Leroy spoke. "Coach, this isn't fair. I'll always finish last. I'm too big." We all laughed. The big man had a point.

"Leave the excuses at the door, Leroy." Coach blew his whistle. "Go!"

We ran silently for at least an hour. We were all exhausted, covered from head to toe in sweat. Some guys could barely move. Leroy Hill finished dead last after giving all he had to stay with the pack. He began picking up balls and placing them in bins at center court. The rest of the guys walked toward the locker room. But one by one, we turned our heads toward Leroy. Grabbing towels and dropping to the floor, we cleaned the court together. A sense of team had been established. Succeed together, fail together, run together, clean together. I looked to the corner of the bleachers. Coach sat there, smiling. This was what he'd had in mind all along.

The first game of my sophomore season was against Lincoln College. We would leave in the morning on a two day trip to Savannah, Georgia. The night before, I went to the gym. After thirty minutes of shooting, I worried about my jump shot. "Release, follow through." My words bounced off the walls in the empty gymnasium.

A voice startled me. "Your elbow's popping out on every shot you miss." Coach Williams approached me.

I tucked my elbow close to my ribs. "All right." I spoke as I shot a few more. "Elbow tucked, release and follow through." I made three in a row.

Coach smiled. "Fundamentals, Tony. That's all this game is."

I cradled the ball under my arm. "Coach Williams? It's no big deal but—do you remember me? Do you remember meeting my brother and me?" I'd been meaning to ask him this question since he took over the team.

"I remember you both. What happened to your brother was a tragedy. He was a great player." He forced a smile. "I guess you made your way back onto that high school team. Picked up that state title too. Pretty impressive comeback, Hope."

He remembered me. "I never had a chance to thank you for that."

He grabbed the basketball from me, palming the leather by his side. "I need you to step up and be a leader this year, Tony." He started dribbling. The ball moved so swiftly between his hands. "In high school, you and your brother thought you two were the best players in the world. That confidence made you better. Every great player needs that swagger. I want to see it this year. That's how you'll lead this team."

I knew exactly what Coach was talking about. In high school, I used to dare defenders to guard me. That confidence vanished the night Mike was shot. "I miss playing with him, Coach. I miss him so much out there."

Coach responded. "I can help you take your gift all the way, Tony. That'll be the best thing you could ever do for your brother. You need to believe in yourself, though." He pulled a jump shot that swished through net. "And keep that elbow tucked."

When we crossed into Georgia two days later, the sound of tires on muddy roads disrupted the silence. Hours passed without a word spoken. We all felt the pressure of the upcoming season. An hour outside of Savannah, Coach Williams instructed our bus driver to pull over. He stood in front of the team. "Are we a basketball team or a bunch of mimes? No one's said a word in here since North Carolina. Did you guys forget how to talk?" No one responded. "Everybody get off!"

We stepped off the bus, expecting the verbal lashing to continue. Instead, we each received an empty basket. Lamar's expression softened. "Pick yourself out a peach." Coach grabbed one from a pile. "We're in Georgia now, best peaches in the world." He took a bite and the guys stared at one another. Had Coach lost his mind? We walked around a small fruit stand and took in the scenery. Everyone was talking now. Big country bugs flew by our heads. Hanging trees blew in the breeze. A farmer named Tyler took us on a walk to the peach trees. I'd never climbed a tree before. So I had Farmer Gibby pick mine.

We all jumped back onto the bus, gripping a fresh peach. I sat in my seat and took a bite. Right away, I realized what Lamar had done. He'd taken our minds off basketball. I listened to comments around the bus. "These things are juicy." C.J. Katz finished his peach in three bites.

Leroy Hill spoke with a full mouth. "They drip down your chin."

Josh tapped me on the shoulder. "You ever had a peach like this, Tony?"

I took a bite and stared at Coach. "No peach trees in Harlem."

Coach Williams agreed. "That's the truth."

We arrived at Lincoln College for our first game of the season. Our first assignment was to clean the peach juice from our hands. Then we'd worry about Lincoln. We were loose when game time arrived. The whistle blew and big Leroy Hill tapped the ball back to me, the starting point guard. I reminded myself of the game plan. "Play with swagger. Penetrate. Attack the defense. Bring it." On the first possession, I brought it to the rim with a two-handed dunk. There couldn't have been a better way to start the season.

Lincoln missed their first couple of shots and never recovered from our 16-2 opening. I finished with twenty points in Coach Williams's first victory. It changed our national ranking from sixteen to eleven. That recognition brought along expectations. We met the challenge, surviving our first eighteen games without a loss. Our season turned down the home stretch. Dreams of perfection kept me awake at night. I looked at our schedule. January 21st, at Trenton, a game I'd circled in red. This was the last roadblock between us and a perfect record.

We entered Trenton's Kennel for the second straight year. Within five minutes, we'd jumped out to a seven-point lead. I dribbled up the floor, turning my head as Gibby hooted for the ball.

Before Josh could shoot, Larry "The Monster" Murphy extended his arm and deflected the ball. I hustled back on defense as Murphy grabbed the rock and began the fast break. I blocked his lane to the hoop. Murphy came charging at me like a bull. Only I didn't get out of his way. I held ground, trying to draw an offensive foul.

Larry wasn't athletic enough to avoid the collision. The truth was, he probably didn't want to. The star linebacker for Trenton's football team loved a good hit. His shoulder blasted me backward and my ribs smacked the hardwood. My ankle twisted beneath his massive body.

The official blew his whistle. "Blocking foul,

fourteen defense." I tried to stand and argue the call, but I crumbled. My leg couldn't support me. A throbbing pain crawled up my ankle. I grabbed Josh's arm for support. When I tried to stand, I failed.

A few of the guys on the bench carried me through a hallway beneath the Kennel. A door opened to the outside and I was led into the back of an ambulance.

The bad news was that we lost that game to Trenton by six. I got the even worse news in the emergency room. My ankle had broken in two places. I would miss the championship tournament.

CHAPTER ELEVEN

WIN OR GO HOME

My broken ankle ended my sophomore season. All I could do was watch as Montana University thumped us in the championship tournament. Two years of college had passed. I'd spent one on the bench, and another nursing a broken ankle.

That summer, I limped home to Harlem with a cast on my leg. When the doctor cut the thing off, I needed rehabilitation. Each morning I would get up early. Not to go to the courts, but to join Mike at Harlem Hospital. He had spent the past twenty-five months rehabbing there.

While I did strengthening exercises on my ankle, Mike attacked bigger problems. Nurses would hook him up to a machine they hoped would awaken his sleeping muscles. He did this for hours, never missing a day. A lot of people gave up after they were delivered the odds of recovery from paralysis—Mike tried harder.

On the last day of my rehab I watched Mike. Two nurses attached wires to his legs. He looked at me and shot a thumbs up, convincing me to believe the same way he did. The nurse turned the machine on. Mike's right leg flinched. I thought I'd imagined it at first. "Did you see that? My leg, T! It moved." I hadn't imagined anything. Mike turned to face the nurse.

She clapped her hands. "It moved alright." She recorded something on her chart.

"Well, what are you waiting for, shock me again!" They did. Again and again. His leg had flinched for the first time in twenty-five months that morning. We waited all day for the second time. But there was no more movement. When we left the hospital Mike was no longer smiling. He was intense, looking at me the way he used to on the basketball court. "I'll walk again, T. I will." As always, I believed him.

After six weeks of Mom's home cooking, my time in Harlem was up. I hopped on a number six train, the most crowded on the tracks in August. I stepped off half an hour later and walked to the apartment I'd be sharing with Josh. Gibby had become one of my closest friends.

I huffed and puffed up eight flights of steep stairs, lugging my bag all the way. When I arrived at our front door, I pounded with my right fist. "Hey

Farmer!" The temperature was around one hundred degrees. "Open up, Gibby, I'm melting out here."

I guessed our apartment wasn't equipped with air conditioning either. When the door opened, Josh was sweating. I did a double take before slapping his hand and greeting him. Gibby looked like he'd been eating too much hay. He was huge! "What happened?" I asked jokingly. "Did you eat Josh?"

He was at least twenty-five pounds heavier than the toothpick who left campus six weeks earlier. "Are you kidding me, Farmer? What are they putting in the corn out there?"

Three months after moving in, our junior season started. Our task was clear: win a national championship. That journey began with a game against Memphis State University. This routine game got tough when Josh and I opened up shooting 2 for 14. Four minutes in, we trailed by eleven to a bad team.

As the point guard, my job was to calm the tempo and be confident. My shooting touch was off, but I could still play with the defense. Two defenders drew close. Calmly, I swirled the ball around my back to avoid their swiping hands. Seconds later I fired a chest pass to my wing. I waited for Josh to bury the jumper. He stood motionless. His confidence was low after a poor one-for-eight start. The shot clock ticked down and Josh threw the ball back to me. I was forced to shoot off balance. My air ball left me embarrassed and annoyed.

On the next play Memphis State scored uncontested. They now lead by thirteen. Coach Williams signaled for a timeout. I came to the bench in a rage. "Take the shot if you're open, Gibson!" I took a sip from a water bottle and threw it to the floor in frustration.

Josh's face turned tomato red. "How about you stop showboating up the floor? Around the back, between the legs—this isn't the Tony Hope Show!"

Coach Williams stepped between us. "Enough finger pointing! Both of you take a seat. Hooper, Jackson, get in there." Coach kicked the scorer's table. He was more upset than I'd ever seen him. "You better start acting like captains, not crybabies."

I retreated to the end of the bench. The next hour and a half was torture. Josh and I sat beside one another as our teammates chased Memphis State up and down the floor. Both of us refused to apologize.

After the defeat, we boarded a plane for a three hour flight to New York. I sat in a window seat. The aisle separated Josh and me. Before the plane took off Coach Williams stood in front of the guys. "That was a terrible loss. You can thank your captains for putting themselves before the team." No one spoke. "On this flight home I want you all to ask yourselves a question. Are we going to succeed together, or fail as individuals?"

I sat with my head leaned against the window. I

felt a tap on my shoulder. "Tony?"

I looked over my shoulder. It was Josh. "Listen Gib, I—"

He cut me off. "Let's squash it, T. Besides, you were right, I should have taken the shot."

"No, I was a jerk. I shouldn't have called you out like that in front of the team." I extended my hand to Josh. "History?"

"Of course. Coach is right, though. We can't win this thing without being on the same page. This is *our* team." He paused. "And this may be our last shot. Leroy's graduating. And we can't win this thing without him. Plus—" He stopped. "Who knows? You could be leaving too." I didn't respond. The team didn't need further distractions. But Josh was right. If everything went well, my junior year *would* be my last. Next year, I would head for the NBA.

I spoke, tiptoeing around my plans. "Well, this is our year then."

Our rocky start didn't ruin a great regular season. We won twenty seven of thirty games, pulling out victory in our last seventeen. Josh and I played in perfect rhythm.

We entered the tournament as the number one ranked team in the country for the first time in UNY's history. Hoffman Arena in Chicago was where our journey began. Our first-round game pitted us against Cheyenne College, a small school in South Dakota. For the first time in three years, I would be part of the playoffs.

Little Cheyenne College knew what was at stake. The soldiers from South Dakota wore their game faces during warm-ups. But a few moments later, when Leroy Hill stepped onto the court, their jaws dropped. The Wheateaters would need stools to defend the giant. He was eight inches taller than anyone on their team.

The game began with a 20-1 burst. We fed the ball into Leroy, who dunked over defenders easily. Cheyenne's Coach, Bobby Alvarez, signaled for timeout after timeout. But there was nothing he could do. Final score—UNY Lightning Storm, 88 Cheyenne Wheateaters, 46.

Getting that win under my belt eased the pressure a bit. But our goal wasn't to win a single game. By the time Cedar Hills College took the floor as our second opponent, Cheyenne was a memory. Victory here would send us to the round of sixteen. Once again, defeat would send us home.

I played amazing against Cedar Hills, scoring a career-high 42 points. We pounded the Coyotes by seventeen. That shooting clinic fueled my confidence as I stepped onto a plane for Dallas and the round of sixteen.

My mental picture of Texas was completely different than reality. Aside from a few country music bars, the Wild West was pretty mild. Although Pennsylvania farm country was a few thousand miles away, Gibby made himself at home. Five minutes after we'd stepped off the plane he was wearing a cowboy hat. He'd tip the thing to every girl we passed.

In our game against Oklahoma Tech, Josh was money. But Ian Epstein, Tech's five-foot-nine sharpshooter, stepped up as well. Josh and Ian traded baskets like baseball cards. Epstein was almost a hero that day. That is, until his jumper clanked off the rim in the closing seconds. Leroy Hill grabbed the rebound to complete a narrow victory. Just one victory separated us from the Last Four, college basketball's grandest stage.

First, we'd have to put a stop to San Diego University's run. After pulling upsets in their first three games, they faced us in the round of eight. We pummeled the "Sunshine Boys" by twenty. Next stop: Los Angeles, sight of the Last Four.

We arrived the following morning. Josh, Leroy, and I spent the day sightseeing. I took a picture next to the HOLLYWOOD sign and Gibby bought another hat. There was nothing anyone could do to wipe the smiles from our faces.

Until game day, that is, when we trailed Upper Nevada with seven minutes remaining. After fouling out, I tried to rally my teammates. I swung a towel in circles above my head. I believed the guys would come through.

When Leroy Hill was slapped in the face by the swinging arm of Upper Nevada's Humphrey Sloan, the game turned. The biggest guy on the floor had become angry. This was bad news for Sloan. Josh began feeding Leroy in the post on every possession. His twelve points in the final six minutes helped us earn a victory. Gibby was right, we couldn't win without our big guy.

That victory set up an exciting title game, the University of New York against Virginia State College. For me, this wasn't just any match-up. The Colonials were led by a pair of familiar faces—Brooklyn's Backcourt. My high school rivals, James Thomas and Walter Randolph, had also brought their team to the title game. This time, the   match-up wouldn't be "Brooklyn's Backcourt vs. The Hope Brothers." Still, basketball fans pulled their seats a little closer as a high school rivalry lived on. The game would be played at the Los Angeles Basketball Center. The 26,000 fans, and the fifty million TV viewers, would be watching closely.

When Josh and I left the interview room we made our way onto the court for warm-ups. Just as we arrived a voice called out from the other end of the floor. "Hey Hope, you're gonna get beat down tonight. Mike isn't here to bail you out this time." I didn't have to look. James Thomas, the point guard I hadn't seen in five years, was *still* talking.

Before the tip, Thomas continued chattering. This time, he targeted Gibby, "You never seen moves like this, country boy. I'm gonna light you up."

We controlled the tip. Josh took two dribbles

and swished a three-pointer. He approached Thomas. "Light *who* up?" The country boy could hang with anyone, both with words and jumpers. He hit his first four shots and did something that even Mike had failed to do—he shut James Thomas up. VSC called a timeout trailing 10–4.

When we came back onto the floor, the Colonials double-teamed Gibby. Silencing him became their main objective. I took this as a challenge. I nailed a few jump shots, a reverse lay-up, and drew two fouls against Randolph. Our lead stretched to 30-17 when VSC called for time.

On the inbound, Thomas fired a laser into Randolph's chest. Walter turned to face me, palming the ball with his right hand. I reached out and poked the leather from his grip. Josh anticipated the break and bolted. Thomas gave chase as I launched a pass. Josh caught the rock over his shoulder and leaped toward a dunk. Thomas rose alongside. Realizing he couldn't block Gibby's shot, he grabbed him. With all his strength, he spun him in mid-air. Josh's huge frame tumbled to the ground. The sound of bone smashing against wood left everyone cringing.

Coach Williams tried to put Tracy Hooper in for Gibby. But Josh refused to leave the floor, waving Hooper back to the sidelines. His right arm hung life-less, yet he pushed forward. He walked to the free throw line, struggling to make one of two foul shots.

Despite Josh's heroics, he wasn't the same

player after that. He could barely shoot. This meant Thomas and Randolph were doubling me. Our eleven-point advantage quickly disappeared. We were down five at halftime and Josh was taken to the hospital.

With Gibby out, I had to find new ways to lead the team. Throughout my life, I'd been feeding the ball to my wing. For twenty-one years, I was the second option. But as I stepped out of the locker room for the final twenty minutes of the season, something happened. Everything became quiet. Normal thoughts about the game stopped. When I picked up a basketball, I swished a jump shot effortlessly. What was that? I thought. My fingers and toes tingled. I thought of Mike in the hospital bed after his accident. "Someday you're going to have a moment where everything will get clear…" A wave of joy rushed through me. My moment had arrived. "You've always been a great player." His voice echoed in my head. I threw up three more jumpers, stepping back a few feet with every shot. Swish, swish, nothing but net.

I guess Thomas continued his trash talking during that second half. I don't really remember. Something strange was happening. I'd entered "the Zone." The moment of clarity Mike predicted had come to pass. *I've always been a great player.*

Virginia State defenders were moving in slow motion. And then, where they moved was irrelevant. I'd become unstoppable. Nearly every shot I took swished through the net. During the final twenty minutes of that game, I attempted seventeen shots and made fifteen. My thirty-three second half points were a playoff record. I'd led UNY to our first Championship in school history.

When you see me today, look at my hand. If I'm not on the court playing, I'm always wearing my ring. It reminds me of my teammates, our season, and the place I went that night.

CHAPTER TWELVE

JUMPING SHIP

Our bus pulled up to campus. There were 10,000 students outside singing the UNY fight song as we arrived. We were national champions and everyone was suddenly a basketball fan.

We made our way through the crowd toward our locker room. Josh threw some of his souvenir hats to the screaming fans. A pretty girl with straight black hair caught his cowboy hat. She placed it on her head and winked at Josh. He pointed at her and tripped on his way to the locker room.

I emptied my locker for the off-season. My last moments as a student-athlete had arrived. After winning the championship, I decided to skip my senior year at UNY for the NBA. But I wasn't stupid. I knew that basketball wouldn't last forever. My business degree was as valuable as my jump shot any day; I would still earn my diploma.

I started my off-season workout two days after returning from Los Angeles. When I arrived at the gym, I lugged a rack of balls from the equipment room. I practiced until my shoes were tired. When I made my way to the drinking fountain, I heard the footsteps of Coach Williams. The snapping of his sandals made his presence certain. Coach was almost always in flip-flops. Blisters and bruises felt better in sandals. Nobody knew this better than "Sweet Feet."

I started to panic as he approached. I'd been avoiding this confrontation for the past two days. Disappointing my hero wasn't something I looked forward to. How was I going to tell him that I wasn't coming back? How could I choose the NBA over another year in his program?

Coach Willliams spoke over his clicking sandals. "Hey Tony." I motioned hello. "Back in here two days after, huh? A lot of guys win one and get lazy. You're still hungry, though. I like that." I felt worse about the news I was about to deliver. I leaned in to get a sip of water. "I wanted to get a head start on next year." The time had come. I couldn't skirt around the truth any longer. "Coach?"

"What's up?" he asked as he spun the ball on his finger.

"I wanted to talk to you about next season." I paused. "I'm going to the NBA." Coach took a shot that barely caught the rim. I'd never seen him miss by that much.

He shook his head. "That wasn't what I thought you were going to say. But that's your choice—" He glared at me sternly. I avoided his eyes.

I broke the silence. "I'm sorry."

"You're ready to play in the NBA, huh?" He asked with his hand on my shoulder.

"Sure." I spoke with confidence.

There was a long pause. Coach waited to speak, formulating something in his head. "OK. Then you shouldn't have any problem beating a forty one year old with creaky knees, right?" He cracked his knuckles loudly.

"What?" I asked, not believing the challenge Coach had put on the table.

"You heard me."

I smiled. "C'mon Coach, you're too old to run with me." I didn't want to beat up on my hero in his old age. The guy standing across from me was a gray-haired replica of the ballplayer he once was.

He took offense. A competitive grumble was in his voice. "We'll play to eleven. If you win, you have my blessing; you *are* ready. If you lose, if I beat you, then you show up to practice next season." Coach was serious, extending his hand to seal the deal. "What do you say?"

I could have walked away and told him my decision was final. I could have headed out the door to the NBA. But how do you turn your back on your hero? I grabbed his hand and shook. "You've got a deal."

He came out of the locker room a few minutes later, wearing high-tops and an old Pride jersey. He stood at the top of the key. "Check it up."

"Don't you need to stretch those old muscles?" I cracked a smile.

Coach stepped up. "Shut up, Hope. I'm ready." He pushed the ball into my chest. His eyes had a focus I'd never seen before. His smile was replaced by a glare. Right then, I realized something— this wasn't Coach Williams anymore. I'd awoken "Sweet Feet."

I checked the ball and dug in defensively. Coach continued to stare me down. I directed my eyes toward his hips, waiting for his move. He took two long, slow dribbles with his right hand. Then his hips shifted left. He was trying to cross me up. My feet shuffled quickly and I extended my hand for the swipe. But I never felt the ball. "Sweet Feet" danced past me, exploding toward an open lay-up. Instead of dropping in a finger roll, he stopped beneath the basket. Then he dribbled back to the top of the key. "That was a free lesson. The next one will cost you a bucket."

I'd never seen a crossover that fast. "Sweet Feet" continued talking. "Didn't think the old man would tie you in knots, did you?" He faked to his left and I flinched, rattled. Coach laughed. "Here I go, son."

He dribbled right at me. I prepared my body for the contact. But Coach stopped on a dime. He nailed a jumper. "One-nothing college hoops." He taunted. "This is just a taste of what an NBA point guard can do to you. You still ready? You still jumping ship?"

I nodded, settling in on defense. Coach dribbled like the ball was part of his hand. He went behind his back, through his legs, through my legs. All the while I swiped and swatted. I never touched leather. I remembered being a kid, watching "Sweet Feet" make opponents look silly. Fumbling, I knew I'd become one of them.

"Sweet Feet" scored at will. I was defenseless. He swished pull-up jumpers, made fancy layups, and his old legs even rose for a slam. Meanwhile, I barely got a shot off. Before I knew what had happened, "Ten-two. Game point, Hope."

I crept up next to him, his back to my chest. He talked to me as he dribbled. "One more year Hope, then you'll be ready."

I swiped and missed. "I'm ready now, old man."

He faked to his left. I slipped and nearly fell. "You need another year, Hope. I believe in you, son. You stay this last year, you'll be a better ballplayer." I swiped at the ball again, "a smarter ballplayer," again I swiped and missed, "and a better person." Coach faded back and shot. The ball danced on the rim and dropped through. "Game over."

I stood quietly and waited for "Sweet Feet" to say something else. Coach patted me on the shoulder and handed me the ball. He turned his back and walked toward the locker room. The gym was silent. All I heard were his squeaking sneakers. Before he walked into the locker room he turned and faced me. "Summer practice starts in three weeks, Hope. I'll see you there."

I'd given Coach my word. And on the first day of practice he did see me there. I averaged career highs in points and assists during my senior season. Once again, we entered the tournament as a favorite to win. But after advancing to the round of eight, we fell asleep against the Durham Dukes. They sent us packing, me for good.

Two months after the season ended, the UNY gymnasium filled up for graduation. I stood in an endless line, waiting for my name to be called. When I stepped up to the podium and received my diploma, Mom started crying. No one in our family had ever graduated college. Two weeks later, Mike was on the podium in Harlem, earning our family's second degree.

CHAPTER THIRTEEN

HARLEM'S HOPE

I came back to Harlem with a college degree. After six weeks of waiting, I nearly slept through draft day. I woke up, threw on a pair of shorts, and ran three miles. I stopped at Mario's Pizza for lunch. Mario shook my hand and slid me a slice of pizza. "Here you go, Tony." He dropped the morning paper on the counter. "You read this?" His thick Italian accent rang through with every word.

I shook my head. "No."

"Check out the back page. I think you'll like it." I turned the paper over. A headline caught my eye: "Pride Trade Gentry, *Hoping* for UNY Standout." The article said that the Pride had traded Lionel Gentry for the number one pick. A smile cracked from the corner of my face. I looked up at Mario. His eyebrows raised below his balding head. "Harlem's Hope playing for the Pride. Not much better than that." He shaped a pile of dough in his hands.

"Not much," I answered. "See you tomorrow, Mario." I threw him a couple of bucks and left.

With the draft nearing closer, I went to the Jungle. I'd been invited to attend the draft in Miami, but declined. The day prior Mike had surgery to repair his left wrist. He'd shattered it during rehab. I wanted to be there for the operation. I also wanted to watch the draft with Mike. But he insisted that I not spend my big day in a hospital room. So I called up Gibby and told him to come to the Jungle. He was also hoping to be drafted.

When I showed up, a group of guys were gathered around Gibby. They laughed as he waved his arms in the air, telling a story. I joined the circle. Nobody told stories like Josh. Once I heard him talking about cows again, I moved away and began shooting.

I looked around at the faces pinned to the fence. I watched them watching me. In twenty minutes, the number one pick would be announced. Beyond the fence, a laundromat with opened doors began attracting a crowd. The television was on. Two kids riding bikes pointed at me. A middle-aged woman waved a sign from her balcony. "MAKE US PROUD, TONY." Kids squirted each other with water guns. Cars drove by, music blasted, and the smells of summer hung in the air. I loved being home.

My focus shifted back to the court. We split up

teams and a pick-up game broke out. I was dribbling at the top of the key when a young defender tried to snake the ball from me. He was overanxious, trying to show me what he could do. I remembered when I was his age, trying to prove to the older guys that I belonged. He swatted at the ball the same way I used to. I crossed over a few times, teasing the youngster. He'd creep closer, and I'd pull back.

After a few easy lay-ups, Josh switched to defend me. I looked over at the kid. The ball hopped out of bounds and I had a second with him. "Keep your eye on the hips, not the ball. Don't swat. And don't let people see you frustrated!" These were the same lessons Lamar taught me. Generations of playmakers passed down knowledge on these courts.

Seconds later, I heard some yelling at the laundromat. "They're about to pick!" I took a jump shot over the top of Josh. I pretended not to feel the excitement. I pretended not to wonder about the New York Pride and their pick. My shot wasn't close. But the rebound bounced into my hands. I was curious as to what was happening across the street. But our game was tied at ten—next basket wins. I eyed the Laundromat. Then I held the ball in front of Josh. I picked up my dribble and pump faked. He bit, leaving his feet. I dropped a soft twelve-footer through the net. Game over.

Trying to remain calm, I sat on a bench near the courts. The noise from the crowd grew louder. I turned in my seat. The small television set was out of my range. A moment later, a pack of kids ran toward me. The smallest in the bunch sprinted onto the court. "The Pride picked Tony Hope!" Then the whole place went crazy.

Josh was the first to run over to me. His hug nearly broke my ribs. "Number one pick! Now aren't you glad I blocked that closet door?"

Without Josh, none of this would have happened. "You're the man, Gibby. Thanks." Josh started to walk away as people gathered around me. In between shaking a hundred hands, I shouted. "Gibson!" He turned back. "I don't care if you are a farmer. We're brothers." And with that comment, I realized where I needed to be. A few miles away, my twin brother was recovering from surgery. Alone, he was watching our dreams come true. I had to share the moment with him.

I sat down on the bench and untied my shoelaces. I was smiling as big as ever. I put on the sandals "Sweet Feet" had given me for graduation. I stood up from the bench, sandals snapping loudly. I reached down to grab my high-tops, but only came up with air. I'd placed my sneakers right beside me. Now they were gone. I checked under the bench, behind the bench, and on the bench. Had someone stolen my shoes? I looked around the crowded courts. Finally, I gave up. I had to see my brother.

I walked toward the exit, where people lined

the fence. I passed by and the links shook wildly. A chant started, "Hope!...Hope!... Hope!"

A little girl tapped me on the shoulder. She pointed toward the sky. I glanced up. Two guys were boosting a kid up the fence. He was holding my sneakers, tying the shoelaces together around the highest part. Now *my* sneakers hung the way "Sweet Feet's" did. Like Harlem's flag.

I spent the rest of that afternoon celebrating with Mike and Mom. We watched as Gibby was selected thirty-third by Dallas. Now he could buy himself a new cowboy hat and wear it full-time. As for me, my wardrobe wouldn't change. Towers Memorial Arena was only ten minutes from Harlem.

My first game was four months later. I sat nervously in my living room that morning. The same living room I'd grown up in. Only now the walls had fresh paint, we had a big screen television, and I sat on a leather couch. I heard the humming of Mike's wheelchair behind me. "What's up?"

He pulled parallel to the couch. "Not much."

"Game day today." I smiled.

"Yeah, I know. I'm excited, you?"

"Yeah. Nervous too." There was an uncomfortable silence. "I want you to be there tonight, Mike. I got you and Mom tickets."

He stared at the floor. "I can't do it, Tony."

"Sure you can. Nobody's gonna see you."

"Yeah, right. When I roll down the aisle, every camera in that place is gonna focus on me. They're gonna tell the story about that night again." His face dropped. I hadn't heard him talk about the accident in a year. "I don't want people thinking 'poor Mike.' I want them thinking about you. This is your night. I'll watch the game from home."

No one was around when I entered the Pride locker room a few hours later. I flipped on the lights and stepped onto a soft blue carpet. Four hours until game time. I moved in front of my locker and stared at my number 14 jersey. The name HOPE was printed across the back.

One by one, my teammates filtered into the locker room. After suiting up we stepped onto the floor for warm-ups. I moved under the basket and rebounded for veteran point guard Maurice Youngkin. Between shots, I'd glance toward the corner of the front row. Empty seats stared back at me. Mom said she was coming. She should have been here already.

I moved to the corner of the bench, a seat reserved for rookies. The ball tipped—still no sign of Mom. Why she was late for my first NBA game? For the next ten minutes I looked like I was watching a tennis match. My head went back and forth from the game to the stands.

When Coach Clark noticed Youngkin breathing heavy and pulling on his shorts he signaled for time. I moved into the huddle, glancing over Coach's shoulder at Mom's seat. Where could she be? Suddenly, I was frozen. Something must have gone wrong with Mike. I searched my brain for a reason Mom was so late. All I could come up with was disaster.

"Hope!" I heard Coach Clark's husky voice. "You ready?"

I wasn't ready, but I had to be. I tore off my warm-ups. "Ready, Coach."

"You're in for Youngkin." He patted me on the back as I passed him and stepped onto the court.

I took a last look toward the stands. My mother was rushing to her seat in the same way I'd imagined. She'd made it after all. And just in time. Now I could focus on beating Chicago. I crouched down and touched the number forty-four on my sneakers. I smiled at my mother. She was pointing up the aisle.

I was unsure what she was doing. I followed the path of her finger. Behind her was the greatest sight of all. Mike wheeled himself through crowds of people toward the front row. He'd made it to my first game. Our eyes met as his chair came to a stop beyond the out-of-bounds line. Mike sat still, staring at me. And then something amazing happened.

My brother grabbed hold of both sides of his wheelchair. The right side of his body began to shake. I watched, mesmerized, as his right leg crept into the air. A moment later, the left side of his body came alive too. A second leg inched into the air, faster than the first. Slowly, he began to emerge from his chair.

Using the strength in his arms, he pushed up from his seat. He stood wobbling for a few long seconds. Mike Hope could move again! Mom grabbed him by the waist and guided him another step. I watched as he plopped down.

His wheelchair sat beside him, vacated. Mike pointed to me from his seat. We shared the look I'd always dreamed of—we'd made it. I was standing on an NBA court realizing our childhood dream. And Mike was on the sidelines, defying *all* the odds.

Dribbling up the floor was easy with Mike there with me. I'd never felt so confident. The basket looked as big as an ocean. I was the captain of a great ship with Mike as my first mate. I heard his voice as I passed the ball to an open teammate.

"I'm on your wing, T. On your wing if you need me."

TEST YOURSELF...ARE YOU A PROFESSIONAL READER?

<u>Chapter 1: Fifteen Hours</u>

Why was Mike nervous about leaving Harlem?

Why didn't Tony go with his brother to the party?

What does the title of this chapter, "Fifteen Hours" refer to?

<u>ESSAY</u>

Tony thinks that Mike had made a terrible mistake by leaving with Nick and Devon. What makes him think this way? Why didn't Tony want his brother hanging out with those guys?

<u>Chapter 2: Shorty</u>

Why did challenging Jason Helms to a game of one on one not seem like one of Tony's smarter ideas?

Describe Tony's defensive theory about staring at his opponents' hips.

At the end of the chapter, Tony says that he has "graduated." What does he mean by that?

ESSAY

Jason Helms got more than he bargained for during his game against Tony. Tony gained respect despite his loss. Has there ever been a time in your life that you "lost but still won?" Explain.

Chapter 3: Locked Out

What two things were east of 1st Avenue and 151st Street?

What led Tony to falsely believe that he deserved special treatment when he showed up for high school tryouts?

What does the chapter's title, "Locked Out" refer to?

ESSAY

Coach Harris told Tony that "he had no respect." Was there a time in your life when you disrespected one of your elders, a coach, a teacher or a parent? What did you learn from this?

Chapter 4: Sweet Feet

Why was Tony surprised when Mike didn't look up at 'Sweet Feet's' window?

What occurred to Tony as he watched his old teammates practice through a crack in the door?

What kept Tony from apologizing to Coach Harris?

ESSAY

When Lamar says that "every dream has a price," what does he mean? What are some of the sacrifices you may have to make to chase your dream?

Chapter 5: Skippin' Out

What statistic proved to Coach Harris that Tony was more than a just a selfish player?

What reasoning did Tony use in trying to persuade Mike not to go to the zoo?

Why is this chapter entitled "Skippin' Out?"

ESSAY

Do you think Tony made the right decision by blocking Coach Harris's path to the locker room? Why or why not?

Chapter 6: Forty-Four

How did the head coach of UNY, Coach Collier, raise the stakes of the state championship?

Why did Tony dislike James Thomas?

Who was the best player on the court during the state championship game? Explain.

ESSAY

In this chapter, Mike struggles to overcome an injury to his knee. He comes back into the game and helps win the state championship. Describe a time in your life when you overcame pain, (physical or emotional), in order to achieve a goal. Was it worth it? Why or why not?

Chapter 7: Invincible

According to Tony, what was the only thing that kept the Hope family from falling apart?

What reason does Mike give Tony for him still being alive?

What seemed important to Tony as he sat in that hospital room?

ESSAY

"Life is a delicate egg, and if you treat it any other way, you'll end up scrambled." Explain this quote using an example in this chapter and an example in your life.

Chapter 8: The Farmer

Who is the "Farmer," and where is he from?

What factors contributed to Tony wanting to leave UNY?

What reasoning did Josh use in trying to convince Tony to stay at UNY?

ESSAY

Tony and Josh are from completely different backgrounds, yet they grow to be friends. What did this teach you? Explain using examples from your life. What did Tony and Josh have in common?

Chapter 9: Stepping Into the Light

Why did the Pitbull players smirk when Tony and Josh entered the game?

Who is "Philadelphia's finest?" Where is he from?

What does the chapter title, "Stepping Into the Light" mean?

ESSAY

In the first line of this chapter, Tony says, "Mom didn't raise quitters." It would have been easy for Tony to return to Harlem and not face the tough road ahead. What would you have done if you had been in Tony's shoes? Explain.

Chapter 10: From Scratch

Why were Tony and Josh nervous when they heard that there was a new head coach?

Why was Coach Williams smiling after everyone helped Leroy clean the gym?

According to Coach Williams, what does every great player need?

ESSAY

In this chapter, Coach Williams teaches his players the importance of being a team. How does he do this? Cite examples from this chapter.

Chapter 11: Win-Or-Go-Home

Why did Tony have a hard time recognizing Josh after he came back for his junior year at UNY?

Why was Tony upset with Josh during the Memphis State game?

Why did Josh feel a sense of urgency to win the national championship during his junior season?

ESSAY

Until Tony entered the Zone, he said that for "twenty-one years he was the second option." Hard work had prepared Tony for this moment. Was there a time in your life when you stopped relying on others and took control yourself? Describe. What prepared you for that moment?

Chapter 12: Jumping Ship

Why was Tony having a hard time telling Coach Williams that he was leaving for the NBA?

What did Tony realize when he saw Coach come onto the court for their game of one on one?

When "Sweet Feet" is dominating Tony, what memory is conjured up inside him?

ESSAY

In this chapter, we see Tony graduate from college and earn a degree. Do you have a subject that you would like to earn a degree in? Why is this your favorite subject? What characteristics do you have that will help you excel in this field?

Chapter 13: Harlem's Hope

Why didn't Tony watch the draft in Miami?

Why did Tony feel for the kid who was overanxious while defending him?

Why did Mike initially refuse to watch Tony's game in person? What do you think led him to come anyway?

ESSAY

Congratulations! You have completed a Scobre book. In light of their journey, tell us what you learned from Tony and from Mike. Which of the Hope brothers seems more like you? Of the two, who was more of an inspiration to you? Explain.